***Is Julie's dream date
going to turn into a nightmare?***

"Oh, Julie," Rosie said. "Are you in pain?"

I nodded. "I'm going to miss the dance."

"Maybe not," Rosie said. "Maybe it's just a sprain."

I shook my head feebly. "The coach says my leg is broken."

Ask your bookseller for these other PARTY LINE titles:

Special party tips in every book!

JULIE'S DREAM DATE

by Carrie Austen

SPLASH™

A BERKLEY / SPLASH BOOK

THE PARTY LINE #6: JULIE'S DREAM DATE is an original pub-
lication of The Berkley Publishing Group. This work has never ap-
peared before in book form.

A Berkley Book/published by arrangement with General Licensing
Company, Inc.

PRINTING HISTORY
Berkley edition/October 1990

A GLC BOOK

Splash and *The Party Line* are trademarks of General Licensing
Company, Inc.
Cover logo and design by James A. Lebbad.
Cover painting by Mike Wimmer.

ISBN: 0-425-12301-4
RL: 5.3

A BERKLEY BOOK® TM 757,375
Berkley Books are published by The Berkley Publishing Group,
200 Madison Avenue, New York, New York 10016.
The name "BERKLEY" and the "B" logo are trademarks belonging
to Berkley Publishing Corporation.

PRINTED IN THE UNITED STATES OF AMERICA

10 9 8 7 6 5 4 3 2 1

One

My sister Laurel is totally into horoscopes. She had read me mine at breakfast that Monday morning. It had said that I would receive good news that day, but as I stood at my locker after my last class I realized that the only news I'd gotten so far was that we were going to have a big history test on Wednesday of the following week. Good news? No way.

As I slammed the locker shut, I saw Allie Gray coming down the hall, swinging her book bag. I waved to her, wondering if maybe she had some news about a party. Not an invitation, but a job. Allie, Becky Bartlett, Rosie Torres, and I have a business called The Party Line. We do kids' birthday parties for parents who have no time to take care of the zillion little things that have to be done. The Party Line does everything from writing invitations to finishing up the last crumb of birthday cake (which happens to be my specialty).

"Let's walk home today, Julie," Allie said. "It's gorgeous out."

THE PARTY LINE

"Then leave it out," I said.

Allie looked blank. "Huh? Leave what out?"

I sighed. I love Allie, but she never seems to appreciate my razor-sharp wit. "It's a joke," I explained. "It's gorgeous *out*—so leave it *out*. Get it? Goldie told me that one." Goldie is my grandmother, who lives in Florida. She knows more jokes than Pee-wee Herman.

Allie still looked puzzled. "Is that supposed to be funny?"

Rosie came up behind Allie. "What's funny?"

"I give up," I said. "What's funny?"

"What Allie was talking about," Rosie said.

"Walking home," Allie said.

"That's funny?" Rosie said.

Allie and I burst into laughter at the look on Rosie's face. I started to explain, but the loudspeaker overhead let out a shriek that would have made a dead dog howl.

"Eee." Rosie scrunched up her face. "That makes my teeth shiver."

Allie stuck her fingers in her ears. "Mouse has a Captain Space ray gun that sounds just like the intercom." Mouse is Allie's little brother. His name is really Jonathan, but Allie calls him Mouse because when he was a baby, the very first noise she ever heard him make was a little mouselike squeak.

"That's it, the school has been taken over by aliens," Rosie said. "That's why the announcements sound like nails screeching across a blackboard.

They'll be able to take over the world because we humans will all be standing around with our hands over our ears."

Rosie's theory was interesting, but in reality the reason that our announcements sound like the special effects in an old science-fiction movie is because the building is being rewired and our principal has been using an ancient PA system until the work is done.

"Shh." Rosie pointed to the loudspeaker. "Listen."

We all stood staring up at the ceiling as if it were the principal himself hanging up there, not a box with a hole in the middle.

For once, the announcements made it worth putting up with all the squawks and feedback. After a couple of plugs for the chess club and the science fair, the principal announced that Canfield Middle School was going to have its first-ever dance for the seventh and eighth graders a week from that coming Saturday.

Normally I never pay any attention to Laurel's astrology nonsense, but as soon as I heard the announcement of the dance the horoscope's prediction flashed into my mind.

"Hey, *that's* the good news!" I blurted out.

Rosie and Allie looked at me as if I were nuts, so I explained about the horoscope.

"I can't wait!" Rosie exclaimed. "Hmm, what am I going to wear?" If you ask me, that was a silly thing for Rosie, of all people, to be worrying about. She has a closetful of great clothes, and she always looks terrific. That day she had on a super tapestry vest, a white shirt with an embroidered collar, and stonewashed jeans.

Just then Allie noticed Becky coming down the hall, and called to her.

"Hey, Becky, want to walk home today instead of taking the bus?"

"Great," Becky called back, and started to run toward us.

Just then the double doors to the library swung open.

"Watch out!" Allie shrieked as two kids loaded down with books came out of the library and walked right into Becky's path. Without slowing down, Becky did a neat sidestep—or it would have been neat if there hadn't been a water fountain on the wall. Her book bag caught on the knob, and she and all her books went flying.

We ran over to where she was sitting rubbing her arm.

"Are you all right?" Allie gasped.

"Well, I'll live," Becky said, surveying the damage. "Besides, I look good in technicolor bruises," she added, getting up and collecting her books. "I should know—I've had enough of them."

That was true. Becky's a kind, generous, and wildly creative person, but she's also a world-class klutz. Her brother, David, calls her a walking disaster area.

"Hey, did you hear what's happening next week?" Becky asked as we walked out the front door of the school and started toward home.

"Yeah. I can't believe we're actually going to have a dance!" I said excitedly.

Becky gave me a strange look. "I wasn't talking about the dance," she said. "I meant the history test."

"I'm not looking forward to that test," Rosie groaned. Neither was I. I'm not the greatest student in the world.

"What do you think Mr. Epstein's going to ask us?" I wondered out loud.

"I made a list of the topics I think are going to be on the test," Allie said. "I can make a copy for you guys if you want."

"Thanks, Allie," I said. Part of the reason Allie gets such good grades is that she's the max when it comes to organization. She says she has to be organized because it's the only way to survive in a family as big as hers. She has four brothers and sisters.

Rosie, Allie, and Becky talked some more about the history test as we walked along, but my mind wandered from the Great Depression to the Great Canfield Middle School Dance.

"I wonder if anybody will have a date for the dance?" I said.

"Anybody?" Rosie said.

"Well, any of us," I said.

"Who needs a date?" Becky said.

"Nobody *needs* one," Rosie said, grinning wickedly, "but if Mark Harris asked her, I bet Julie wouldn't mind having one."

Of course Rosie knew I had a crush on Mark, because she's my very best friend. Becky and Allie knew, too. But Rosie didn't have to say out loud that I wanted a date with him! I felt my face get hot, which meant it was also getting red. I shrugged and tried to sound casual.

"Well, if you got asked to a dance, wouldn't you want it to be someone who wasn't a total dweeb?"

Becky just snorted. She really isn't into boys yet. But Allie smiled and got a kind of faraway look on her face. She's interested in Dylan Matthews, another boy in our class, and I bet she was thinking about whether he'd be at the dance.

The others started discussing which of the boys we knew might actually show up at the dance, but I couldn't drag my thoughts away from Mark. He is one of the cutest boys in school—he's got gorgeous blue eyes and wavy dark-brown hair. He even gets a dimple in his cheek when he smiles.

But that's not why I like him. He's a radical Red Sox fan, and so am I. Okay, I'll be honest—it isn't just that he's a Red Sox fan. I think I'd like him even if he rooted for the Yankees. I mean, he's *that* cute. I think he likes me, too. He's never actually said so, but we're partners in biology lab, and when you get good vibes from someone you're dissecting a frog with, it's got to mean something, right?

I'd give anything if he'd ask me to the dance, I thought. I started thinking about the new dress I'd get if he did ask me—blue, probably, because I have blond hair and blue eyes. I'd ask Rosie to help me with my hair and makeup. She's great at things like that, despite what happened the last time she tried to give me a makeover. One day we had all been hanging out in Becky's attic and Rosie talked me into letting her cut my hair. I got nervous when I saw how much hair she was cutting off, and I made her stop so I could see what she was doing. It was so uneven and gross-looking that I burst into tears, and so did Rosie. It all turned out okay, though— Rosie, Becky, and Allie took me to a salon and I had it recut. I still get compliments on how good I look with short hair.

My mind drifted back to the dance. I've always been athletic, and dancing just seems to come naturally to me. *I bet Mark is a good dancer, too,* I thought. *He's got great moves on the basketball court, and I can just see the two of us on the dance floor. . . .*

"Earth to Berger," Rosie said. "Julie Berger, come in, please."

"Huh?" I said.

"You must have been a million miles away, from the look on your face," Allie said.

"Betcha I know where she was," Rosie teased.

I was saved from having to think up a smart answer to that one because Becky said, "Hey, I wanted to show you a clown routine I saw on TV the other day. I think we can use it for our parties."

Clowning around is serious business to us, because of The Party Line. The whole idea for a party business started with a clown.

Allie's mom had hired a clown to perform at Mouse's fourth-birthday party, but the clown got sick and didn't show up. Mrs. Gray didn't know what to do with a houseful of cranky four-year-olds, and that's where we came in. Allie and Becky dressed up as clowns, Rosie drew cartoon faces on balloons, and I organized games. We had a blast doing it, and the kids seemed to have a great time. The next day Allie got a call from the mother of one of the party guests, who asked if we would do a party for her child. That's all it took—The Party Line was born.

"Are you guys coming over to my house?" Becky asked the three of us.

"I'll come," Allie said. "It would be great if we could learn some mime routines, too. I think the kids would really like that."

I looked at Rosie. "Well?"

"Do we have any Party Line business?" Rosie asked.

Becky shook her head. "No. I just wanted to see what you think of the clown routine, and I guess I'll see if Allie can turn me into a mime."

Rosie and I both laughed.

"A mime doesn't talk," Rosie said. "You'll never make it, Becky."

Becky stuck out her tongue at Rosie, then lifted her nose in the air.

"You just passed the first test, Becky," I said. "You told Rosie off and didn't say a word."

Becky grinned. "See, Rosie? I can do anything!" As she spoke she tripped on the sidewalk and would have given herself a real clown nose, but she caught herself just in time and didn't even drop her book bag.

"Nice save, Becky," I said.

Two

"Why are you guys running?" Rosie called to Allie and Becky.

They had gotten way ahead of us in spite of the fact that Becky kept going into a duck-waddle walk. It was part of the clown routine that she had been telling us about. It sure looked funny from where Rosie and I were walking, and several people on the street smiled at Becky as they passed.

Rosie and I had fallen behind Allie and Becky because I was asking Rosie for advice on what to wear to the dance. We ran to catch up with them at the corner.

"I've only got an hour before I have to go work at the Moondance," Becky said. Her mother and stepfather run the Moondance Café on the first floor of an enormous old Victorian house, and the Bartletts live upstairs. Becky's mother runs the business end of the restaurant, her stepfather does most of the cooking, and she and her brother help out in the kitchen and the dining room.

The trouble is, Becky's so accident-prone that her parents are a little skeptical about letting her in the dining room when there are customers around. A few months ago, she was carrying a fluffy chocolate cake from the restaurant's kitchen to the dessert cart in the dining room when she tripped over a pocketbook one of the customers had put on the floor next to her chair. Well, you can guess what happened—the chocolate cake wound up in someone's lap, and Becky was banished from the dining room for a while. But recently her parents have started letting her help prepare the vegetables and stuff for the salad bar.

"I think Julie and I are just going to go back to my house for a while," Rosie said. "We'll see you guys tomorrow, okay?"

We started across the park. I looked over my shoulder and saw Becky still duck-walking along the sidewalk, Allie strolling calmly beside her. I looked at Rosie and smiled, thinking how glad I was not to have ordinary, boring people for best friends.

"Hi, Rosie. Hi, Julie," Rosie's mother called as we walked into Rosie's house. Mrs. Torres was sitting in the kitchen, looking at samples of hair accessories. She owns Cinderella, one of the trendiest boutiques in town, and uses Mondays, when the shop is closed, to order accessories and clothing for the store.

Mrs. Torres held up two headbands, one decorated

with tiny dried roses and lace and the other covered with woven, dyed straw.

"Which do you like, Rosie?" she asked. Rosie has such good taste in clothes and colors that her mom often asks her advice.

Rosie paused and looked at the two of them. "Well, I like them both, but the one with the roses is sort of fancy. Didn't you order a lot of simple, colorful clothes last month?"

"You're right, and the straw headband would go with a lot of those outfits," Mrs. Torres said. "Oh, and I stopped at the bakery and got some of those gingerbread cookies you like, Rosie. Help yourselves—there's milk in the fridge."

"Thanks, Mom. Hey, is that anti-Dracula chicken I smell cooking?"

I must have looked puzzled, because Rosie laughed and explained, "It's my father's favorite. We call it anti-Dracula because it's got enough garlic in it to keep you vampire-free for months."

Rosie poured us some milk and I picked up the bag of cookies.

"We'll be upstairs in my room in case anyone calls," Rosie said.

"Who'd call us?" I said as I trailed Rosie up the steps.

Rosie went into her room and flopped on the bed.

"Maybe Casey Wyatt will call to ask you to the dance," she said with a mischievous glint in her eyes.

I couldn't let that one pass. Casey Wyatt is the most obnoxious boy in school. He never lets me forget I'm wearing braces—his favorite names for me include "Metal Mouth" and "Jaws."

I grabbed one of the dozens of pillows Rosie has on her floor and tossed it at Rosie's head. She ducked and came up armed with a pair of giant red velvet lips. I caught the lips and hugged them next to my face.

"I didn't know you cared," I said.

We both collapsed in giggles, but after a moment Rosie turned thoughtful. "You know, I should do a color chart on you. Those lips are too red for you. Here, try this purple next to your face." Rosie picked up a pillow that looked like a bunch of grapes and tossed it over to me.

I held the grape pillow next to my cheek. "I feel like I'm in an underwear ad," I joked. I crossed my eyes and stuck out my tongue. "Fruit of the Loony."

Rosie laughed. "No, seriously. Want me to do your colors? That way you'll know what color dress to buy for the dance."

"Sure," I said.

Rosie rummaged around in her top drawer and finally came up with a bunch of colored scarves. She put a yellow one around my neck, then shook her head.

"Yellow's definitely not your color. With your blond hair you'd look like a banana. Mark would take one look at you and split."

That cracked us both up. We laughed until we were almost crying.

Rosie was the first to calm down. She took a red scarf and wrapped it around my neck. She stepped back and took a critical look at me.

"Not bad. Blonds can wear certain shades of red."

"Red? I wanted to get a blue dress."

Rosie dropped the red scarf on the floor and tied an azure silk scarf around my neck instead. She smiled. "It's you. Tell you what—let's go shopping later this week."

We agreed that we'd go to the mall over the weekend, and Rosie would show me some different things to do with my hair. We finished the cookies, and then I headed home.

As I walked along the sidewalk I couldn't help thinking about the dance again. Rosie was enthusiastic about going, but she didn't seem to care whether anyone asked her to go or not. That didn't surprise me, because she loves to flirt. But the more I thought about it, the more I wanted to go with Mark.

Mark and I had sort of been good friends ever since we had been on the same softball team at a party The Party Line had thrown for Casey Wyatt. Why we would ever have given a party for Casey is a story in itself—it was really all a mistake, because I had taken the job thinking it was for a younger brother Casey didn't have. But we'd agreed to do the job, and the softball game we'd planned had turned into a boys-against-girls contest.

Anyway, ever since then Mark and I had talked a lot in bio and helped each other with the lab reports, but we had never talked much outside class or gone anywhere together after school. The dance would be the perfect chance for us to get to know each other better.

But was Mark even going to go to the dance, much less ask me to go with him?

Three

The next day Rosie and I were standing in the cafeteria line contemplating the special of the day: fish fillet, carrot salad, and jello.

Rosie shuddered. "No wonder so many kids sneak over to the taco place across the street. Who can eat this stuff?"

"It really isn't that bad," I said, loading up my tray. "The carrot salad's got lots of raisins in it." My friends are always amazed at what—and how much—I can eat. What they say about me is absolutely true. I'm a traveling stomach.

Rosie finally settled on a grilled cheese sandwich and we went over to join Becky and Allie at our usual table.

"Rosie, you should definitely be on the decorating committee for the dance," Allie said. "Remember those flower centerpieces you made for the party at Pine Villa? Everybody thought those were great."

"Allie and I have already signed up for the entertainment committee. We get to pick the D.J. for the dance and decide what kind of music we want him to play," Becky said, her meat-loaf sandwich in one hand. Living over a restaurant definitely has advantages. Becky usually brings leftovers from the Moondance for lunch, and Russell's herbed meat loaf was not the usual gray stuff you think of when you think leftovers.

We discussed the music they wanted to choose for the dance—lots of Vermilion, who is Allie's favorite, and Jesse Barrett, whom Becky really loves. Of course, they'd pick lots of Bastille, too—for Rosie. Rosie showed us a few quick sketches she'd just made of centerpieces for the food tables. She told us that she was thinking about using ordinary boxes and cans of different sizes and shapes and covering them with paper and glittery triangles and circles, so that they'd look like wild, geometric space-art.

All of a sudden Becky dropped her apple on the table.

"I can't believe I forgot to tell you guys about the job I got for us!" she gasped.

"The Party Line has another job? That's great. I can really use the money," Rosie said.

"I got a call last night from Mrs. Turner. Her daughter, Ellie, is going to be eight, and she wants us to do her party."

Just then the bell rang. We all tossed our trash in the garbage pail, and as we headed toward our next class Becky said, "Can you all come over to my house after school today? The party's a week from Saturday, and we should get started buying the supplies and planning the games."

We all agreed to meet at Becky's after school, and it was only as I was sitting in math class that afternoon that I realized Becky had signed us up for a party on the same day as the dance.

Later that day Rosie and I climbed the stairs into Becky's attic and saw her sitting cross-legged on an old rug, her history book open in front of her.

Party Line meetings are always held in Becky's attic, which is a great old space filled with dusty trunks and old furniture. We cleaned it up a little and brought up some rugs and pillows to sit on. It's especially great because it's our own place—no one else ever goes up there.

"Hi, guys," Becky said. "Did you see Allie?"

"No, where is she?"

"She's running an errand for her mother. We'll wait for her to—"

Just then the door opened and Allie bounced up the steps. "Am I the last one?" She looked at the rest of us. "Sorry I'm late." She had her notebook under one arm and a bag of pretzels under the other.

I snagged the bag and crunched down on a pretzel. "Can we get started now? I think there's going to be a problem with this job."

Allie flipped open her notebook and fished a pen out of her pocket. Becky calls her the Party Line perfectionist, because Allie makes up an information sheet for each party so that we don't forget anything.

"Okay," Becky said, putting on her most presidential manner. (She's the president because the idea for starting The Party Line was hers.) "Like I said at lunch, this party is for Ellie Turner, and it's a week from Saturday."

Allie didn't write anything down. She looked at Becky, then at Rosie and me.

"That's the twenty-ninth," Becky said.

"We know what date it is, Becky," I said. "I'm sure you know, too."

"What are you talking about?" Becky said.

"The school dance is a week from Saturday, too," Rosie said.

"So what?" Becky said. "The party's in the afternoon. We should be through in plenty of time."

Allie looked at Rosie and me and then shrugged. "I guess she's right," she said. "Even with all the cleaning up, we're usually done by five-thirty or six."

"But the dance starts at seven-thirty!" I reminded them.

"How long does it take to change your clothes?" Becky asked.

I couldn't believe Becky was being so casual about the dance. "It's not just the time between the party and the dance," I said sharply. "What about all the work we have to do to get ready for the party?"

"Come on, Julie," Allie said. "We all pitch in on the party work. It's never been that big a deal."

"Allie's right," Rosie said.

"I still think you should have checked it out with us before you accepted the party, though," I said crossly.

"Who accepted the Casey Wyatt party without asking us first?" Becky shot back.

"Fine, blame it all on me," I snapped. It came out sounding nastier than I meant it.

Allie looked shocked at my outburst. "I think we can work it out, Julie. After all, Becky, Rosie, and I have a lot of work to do for the dance in addition to the stuff for Ellie's party. We have to get all that done in the next ten days, too," she pointed out mildly. She looked at Rosie worriedly.

Rosie glanced at Allie, then turned back to me. "You know, we could probably combine our trips to the mall, and shop for party supplies at the same time we look for a dress for you for the dance."

I knew Allie and Rosie were right, and I knew I shouldn't have snapped at Becky. But I still felt upset, and I wasn't sure why.

Allie turned back to her notebook. "Becky, did Mrs. Turner say what kind of party she wanted for Ellie?"

With a final glare at me, Becky swiveled around to face Allie. "She said she'd leave it up to us. I mentioned that we had been working on a new clown routine, and she said that sounded just fine."

"Maybe we could do a circus theme," Rosie mused, pulling out her sketch pad and some colored pencils.

Rosie's a terrific artist, and she always carries a few art supplies around with her.

"When I was younger Russell used to make these great clown sundaes for me and David," Becky suggested. "You take a scoop of ice cream, put a sugar cone in upside down to make a clown hat, and use candies to make eyes, a nose, and a mouth."

"That sounds great!" Rosie said, looking up from her sketch pad. "Hey, Secretary, are you getting all this down?" She was talking to me. I'm the official secretary, and I'm supposed to take notes at all our meetings.

"What? Oh . . . uh, I didn't bring a notebook. Rosie, can I borrow some paper and a pencil?" I stammered.

"I guess you were too busy daydreaming about Mark Harris to remember our business meeting," Becky said. She was trying to make a joke, but it really bugged me.

"I'm here, aren't I? And you can just leave Mark out of it," I returned, without looking at her.

There was an awkward silence for a few moments. Then Allie and Rosie started discussing the rest of the menu and the games we could organize for the kids, while Becky and I shot angry glances at each other.

"Julie, you can juggle really well," Rosie said gently. "How about teaching the kids a few basic juggling moves?"

"Yeah, that would be great," Allie chimed in.

"Okay," I agreed, a little sullenly.

Nobody could think of anything more to say after that. Normally we hang out in Becky's attic for a little while after meetings, just talking and eating. But Becky and I were avoiding each other's eyes, and I could tell that no one felt like staying.

Rosie finally broke the silence. "I should be getting home," she said. "I need to practice for my piano lesson. It's not until Thursday afternoon, but my teacher was annoyed with me last week because I'd spent more time sketching than practicing scales."

We all trooped downstairs, and Rosie and I set off in one direction while Allie went the other way.

After we'd walked for a few minutes, Rosie said quietly, "We have to come up with a few more ideas for Ellie Turner's party. We really didn't get a lot done today."

"Yeah," I said.

We walked in silence for another few minutes, and then I said, "Rosie, are you sure you don't mind looking for a dress for me when we go shopping for party favors?"

Rosie brightened. "No problem," she said. The rest of the way home we talked about how I might wear my hair to the dance.

Just as I was turning into my driveway, Rosie stopped.

"Julie, I'm sure that we'll have enough time after Ellie's party to get ready for the dance. I'll be helping you, so it won't even take an hour," she said comfortingly.

"Right," I muttered.

That's easy for her to say, I thought as I shut the door and walked upstairs. *Rosie always looks good, no matter what. But it's going to take more than an hour to turn me into someone Mark wants to dance with instead of throw a softball to!*

Four

I was in my bedroom that evening, trying to concentrate on my history assignment, but I wasn't getting very far. Dizzy, my cat, kept nudging me to scratch her ears, and my mind kept going back to the fight we had almost had in Becky's attic that afternoon.

"It wasn't my fault," I said out loud. Dizzy blinked and switched her tail.

I still didn't think that Becky should have booked a party for the day of the dance without checking with the rest of us. I know that Becky sometimes goes full steam ahead with one of her ideas without thinking about the consequences. A lot of the time that works out really well—The Party Line is a good example of one of Becky's ideas that turned out just fine.

But other times it *doesn't* turn out okay. Like the time she put raisins in the potato salad at the Moondance. Or when she booked Ellie Turner's party.

Dizzy dug her nose into my neck and purred into my ear. *At least my cat loves me,* I thought.

I heard the phone ring, but I didn't move, even though it was eight o'clock, the official time for Party Line calls. After meeting that afternoon I didn't expect the telephone chain to be in operation.

When we first started The Party Line we came up with the idea of a phone chain. If I have any Party Line news I call Allie, she calls Becky, and Becky calls Rosie. This way we each have to make only one call, instead of three, to let everyone know what's going on. It keeps all our parents happy. And in my case, it keeps my sisters happy, too. I have two older sisters who are practically welded to the phone. They get so upset whenever I spend more than thirty seconds talking to any of my friends that I figure they think Alexander Graham Bell invented the telephone just for them.

Suddenly my bedroom door banged open. Laurel stood in the doorway, pulling on her jacket.

"Julie, are you deaf?" she shouted.

"I will be if you keep yelling like that," I said.

"It's Rosie," she said, ignoring me.

I headed for the phone in the upstairs hallway. Laurel went downstairs, yelling over her shoulder, "Mom and Dad went to pick out tile for the kitchen floor, they'll be back in half an hour. Heather's at Paula's and I'm going to study at Mary Jo's if anyone wants to know."

I picked up the phone with a sigh of relief. At least

my sisters wouldn't be hanging over my every word, asking when I was going to hang up.

"Hello?" I said.

"What's going on over there, Julie? I heard Laurel yelling," Rosie said.

"Just a normal night at the Bergers'," I said. "What's up?"

"Not much. How're you?" Rosie asked.

I slid down the wall and sat on the hall floor.

"I'm okay," I said.

There was a pause at the other end of the line. Then Rosie said, "You were really upset when you left the meeting this afternoon, weren't you? I just wanted to call and say I was sorry about what happened."

"Why should you be sorry?" I said. "You didn't do anything."

"I feel funny about the way we left things. None of us has ever left a meeting mad before."

"That's because Becky never acted like the boss of the world before."

"Julie!" Rosie said. "She's The Party Line president."

"So? Does that mean she can't do anything wrong?" I said. "She had no right to make that crack about Mark."

"She got a little carried away, that's all."

"Well, I still think she has to ask the rest of us before she goes making big decisions."

"Julie, she only took a party job. Remember last

weekend you and I were wishing we had a party to do, because we could use the money? And I think Becky meant it when she said she didn't think it would interfere with the dance."

"Whose side are you on, anyway?" I was close to shouting.

"I didn't think The Party Line had sides," Rosie said quietly.

I didn't say anything for a minute. Rosie was right: we didn't have sides. Rosie was my very best friend, but Becky and Allie were next.

Dizzy, who had come over to sit near me, turned her back on me and marched into my parents' bedroom.

"Dizzy agrees with you," I said.

"Smart cat." Rosie laughed.

"I guess maybe I should have chilled out this afternoon instead of blowing up at Becky," I said.

"Oh, well. You know Becky. She won't hold it against you," Rosie said.

"Rosie, uh, about the party . . ."

"Um . . . yeah?" Rosie hesitated. She sound a little uncomfortable.

"I think we should go ahead with it," I said.

I could hear Rosie sigh.

"Listen," I went on, "I still think it's dumb to do a party on the same day as a school dance, but if Becky promised Mrs. Turner, The Party Line can't go back on it."

"I'm so glad to hear you say that," Rosie said. "I

felt really bummed out after this afternoon. Listen, we've got to have another meeting tomorrow. We didn't get enough accomplished today."

All of a sudden I felt angry again. "So? That's because Becky was more interested in picking on me than in getting any work done."

"That's not true, Julie, and you know it," Rosie said sharply. "Becky didn't mean it the way you took it."

"Okay," I said after a moment. "Do you want me to call Allie and tell her about the meeting, or did you three decide it already?"

"No," Rosie said. "I mean, yes, you have to call her. I talked to her before, and we agreed we'd have to have another meeting, but we decided if you couldn't make it tomorrow we'd do it when you could be there." Rosie drew a deep breath.

"You mean you thought you couldn't have a meeting without me?" I asked.

"Can you have a pizza without pepperoni?" Rosie said. "Or a hot fudge sundae without whipped cream?"

"Stop," I said. "You're making me hungry."

"Well, call Allie before you start making a sandwich," Rosie said. "She might be in bed by the time you get finished eating."

I laughed. Rosie knows how enormous my appetite can be. "Did I tell you about the scrumptious one I invented last week? My dad named it Cold Cut Catastrophe. You take—"

"Spare me, Julie," Rosie said. "I just had dinner. Call Allie and tell her it's a go on the meeting tomorrow. See you in the morning."

"Bye, Rosie."

I felt a little better as I hung up the telephone. Rosie always knows when to be serious and when to lighten up—I guess that's why she's my best friend.

But I still had to call Allie. Reluctantly, I picked up the phone and punched in her number.

"Hi, Allie? It's Julie," I said when I heard her voice. "I just talked to Rosie and she told me—well, I think we should have another meeting tomorrow."

"Oh. Um, yeah. I think that's a g-good idea." Allie stutters a little whenever she's nervous or uncomfortable. Right then I was feeling pretty awkward, too. After all, Allie and Becky are very best friends, and so I figured Allie was upset with me for having snapped at Becky.

"Is it going to be at Becky's after school tomorrow?" I said finally.

"Yes. C-can you bring the notes you took today?" Allie said.

"Sure." There was another pause. "Well, bye."

"Bye."

I sighed, the receiver still in my hand. I hoped the next day's meeting was going to go better than that afternoon's. It couldn't be much worse.

Five

The four of us had lunch together the next day, like we always do, but we were a little quieter than usual. Nothing really bad happened, though, so as the four of us started walking to Becky's after school I was hoping that everything would soon be back to normal.

But Allie was bursting with some news. She started to tell us in front of school, but a bunch of guys came whizzing past on bikes and she clammed up. Casey Wyatt was one of the boys. He made like he was heading right for me, but I didn't move. I think I would have let him hit me before I let him think I was afraid of him.

He swerved at the last minute. "Sorry, Berger," he yelled. "I have a magnet in my pocket and it wanted to get at your braces." He laughed.

Becky called, "I think you just want a kiss from Julie."

"Becky!" I screamed. "Don't even joke about that." I looked around quickly to see if Mark Harris

Julie's Dream Date

was riding with Casey. They're cousins and usually hang out together, but I didn't see Mark anywhere.

"Did you see the look on Casey's face when Becky said he wanted to kiss Julie?" Allie was laughing. "Like he'd bitten into a wormy apple."

I made a face. "Casey would probably *like* wormy apples."

"He's a creep," Rosie said. "Allie, what were you going to say before Creepy Casey came along?"

"It can wait until we're in the attic," Allie said.

We almost ran to Becky's house.

"Okay," Becky said as she dropped her book bag on the attic floor. "What's the big secret?"

Allie smiled at us. "W-well," she began. Her face was pink.

"It's only us," Rosie said gently.

"I got invited to the dance," Allie said quickly, beaming.

"You what?" I said. I couldn't believe my ears.

"All *right*!" Rosie hugged Allie.

"Who?" Becky asked.

"Dylan," Allie said.

"Allie! When did this happen! I don't believe you're going out with a boy! What did he say? What did you say?" Becky asked.

Allie laughed. "One question at a time, Becks. He just asked me a few minutes ago. I was standing at my locker. I looked up, and there he was. He seemed kind of nervous, but I was pretty nervous, too. He said hi, and I said hi, and then we talked about the history test for a little while, and then. . . . well, he asked me if I wanted to go to the dance." Allie blushed again.

"You're going, aren't you?" Rosie demanded.

Allie beamed. "Yes!" She practically shouted.

Becky grinned and shook her head. "Gray, I still think you're crazy. I bet Dylan's going to step all over your feet. I can just see it now." Becky danced around the attic, stumbling and limping as if a hippopotamus were stomping on her toes.

Allie couldn't help giggling. "Cut it out, Becky. I'm sure Dylan's a great dancer."

Becky stopped galumphing around the room and giggled, too. "I know. I'm just teasing, Allie."

"Allie, want me to do a makeover on you?" Rosie suggested.

"Sure," Allie agreed.

"Great! Hey, Julie, isn't this the max?"

I hadn't said a word since the three of them had started chattering about Dylan and the dance. I didn't know what was going on inside me. Part of me felt happy for Allie, because she was one of my best friends. But part of me was jealous because Allie had been asked to the dance, and I hadn't. I was still a little hurt that Rosie hadn't stuck up for me yesterday. I knew it was unreasonable, but I felt like she'd taken Becky's side. And now here she was offering to give Allie a makeover. I knew I was being stupid and that I shouldn't feel that way, but I couldn't help it. I swallowed hard.

"Julie? Are you okay?" Rosie asked, peering at me.

"Uh . . . yeah, sure."

Becky banged on an old trunk. "Okay, enough about the dance. We came here because we have a party to do, remember? Yesterday we decided on a circus theme. Julie, can you read back the notes you took at yesterday's meeting?"

Suddenly I got a sick feeling in my stomach. "I forgot to bring the notes," I mumbled, looking down.

There was a pause, then Becky sighed. "Well, I think we were going to make clown sundaes and teach the kids how to juggle. I think we were also going to do something like that clown routine I saw on TV, right?"

"That's right," Rosie said. "And I can do some balloon animals. I'm getting pretty good at it." She had bought a craft book that includes instructions on how to twist long, thin balloons into animal shapes. They're really cute, and kids love them.

"Julie?" Becky said loudly, sounding annoyed.

"Huh?" I hadn't been listening. "What?"

"Can you do some tapes of circus music?"

"Sure," I said. I usually make a tape to fit the party theme.

"Hey, Julie, remember that game we were playing with Mouse and Mike at my house the other day?" Allie said. Mike was her ten-year-old brother.

"You mean Monkey See, Monkey Do?" I said, smiling. I had stood in front of Mike and Mouse, imitating an animal, and then I had the kids imitate me.

"Yeah," Allie said. "Mouse stands in front of the mirror all the time imitating the animals you did for them. Mom thinks it's a great game because it's fun and educational, too."

Allie gave me a big smile, and I gave her a quick one in return. I looked down at the floor. I was still a little envious of Allie because Dylan had asked her to the dance, and I felt bad about that.

"Okay, Julie can do that game," Becky said. "We can give prizes for the one who does the best imitation of a monkey, a lion, a kang—"

"Look," I interrupted her, "instead of going through the whole zoo, if I'm going to lead that game, why don't I just decide what animals to do? I'll pick out the prizes, too."

"Okay, Julie," Becky said, giving me a disgusted look. "Don't get all bent out of shape."

"Are we all going shopping for party stuff together?" Allie asked. "That's half the fun of giving the parties."

"That's right," Rosie said. "Let's go after dinner tonight."

"Oh, I can't tonight," Allie said. "I have to baby-sit Mouse. How about tomorrow?"

"I have piano lessons on Thursdays," Rosie said.

"I couldn't make it then, either," Becky said. "Ms. Dorner wants to see me after school Thursday." She grimaced. "I know why. She wants me to enter my recipe for tomato-soup cupcakes in the school district's bake-off."

"That's not a bad idea," Allie said. "I know it sounded like a weird thing to make in home ec class, but those cupcakes were really good! I mean, before we knew what was in them."

"Hmm," Becky said thoughtfully.

"Yeah, Becky, go for it," Rosie said. "Those cupcakes were a lot better then Nick Melton's chocolate-chip pizza." She shuddered at the memory.

"Hey, that wasn't so bad," I said. I like chocolate chips in—or on—anything.

"Look, let's get back to the shopping," I went on. "I have to get home early today."

We decided to divide up the shopping. Rosie and I would go on Friday afternoon to get the paper goods and the prizes, and Becky and Allie would get the food early the next week. As soon as that was settled I said I had to leave. Rosie said she would walk with me, but Allie was going to stay at Becky's a little longer.

"I really can't wait to go the mall on Friday," I said to Rosie after we had walked a block.

"We go to the mall two or three times a week," Rosie pointed out. "What's so special about this trip? Besides, when we were at Becky's you didn't look too thrilled about the idea of going shopping." She paused a moment, then added, "You know, you looked like you had a mouthful of fishhooks all during the meeting. Are you upset because Allie has a date for the dance?"

How could I admit to my best friend that I was jealous for no good reason?

"Come on, Rosie," I said. "Why should I be jealous? It's just that I had a headache and I didn't feel like sitting around Becky's attic when we'd already decided what we had to do for Ellie's party."

"Mmm. Are you feeling better?" Rosie asked.

"Yes," I lied. The truth was, I was feeling worse than ever.

Six

Thursday started out pretty rotten. First of all, I hadn't slept well during the night, because I kept having strange dreams in which Rosie, Allie, and Becky couldn't see me. I kept shouting and screaming and stepping in front of them, but they never seemed to notice me—or to notice that I wasn't around.

Then I overslept, probably because all those weird dreams had tired me out. I got up five minutes before I had to leave to catch the bus, and wouldn't you know it—Laurel was in the bathroom.

I banged on the door, but all she said was, "Go away!"

"Laurel, I'm late and you've got another half-hour before you have to leave. Come on, I've really got to take a shower."

She came out even more grumbly than usual, but I ignored her and dashed into the shower. I don't usually dawdle in the shower, but that day I was out in two minutes flat.

Leaving my hair wet, I threw on some jeans and an off-white sweatshirt with a Florida scene printed on it. The only clean socks I could find were some old ones with large red polka dots on them, but I didn't have time to be fussy. I threw them on, jumped into my sneakers, grabbed my book bag, and made it to the bus with three seconds to spare.

But that wasn't all. Of course I'd forgotten my English homework, and Ms. Lombardi picked that day to make an issue out of it.

By the time I got to the lunchroom, I was really in a bad mood. I searched through my pockets, and found nothing.

"Allie! Am I glad to see you," I said, seeing her at the table where the four of us always sit. "I was really late this morning, and forgot to take any money for lunch. Do you have any money I can borrow?"

Allie rummaged through her purse, but found a grand total of only forty-three cents.

"Well, that will get you an apple, but we all know you can't survive on just that," she remarked cheerfully. "Wait a minute—here comes Becky. She'll probably have some money."

Seeing Becky, my stomach sank. I remembered how unpleasant The Party Line meeting had been the day before, and I didn't especially want to look like a fool in front of her.

"Oh, uh, well, that's okay, Allie. I just remembered Rosie owes me a few dollars, so I'll wait and get it from her."

Becky looked at the two of us as she sat down at the table. "So," she said after a few seconds, "where's Rosie?"

"I don't know," I muttered.

Allie and Becky started talking about the movie they had rented the night before. I wasn't paying attention; I was so hungry my stomach hurt, and Rosie wasn't anywhere to be found.

I looked around the lunchroom. After a few moments I spotted Mark Harris eating lunch on the other side of the room with Casey Wyatt and a few other boys. I got glummer and glummer as I watched him, imagining that he was telling his friends he wouldn't be caught dead at some dumb dance.

Finally Rosie breezed in, looking happy.

"Hi, guys. Sorry I'm late," she said. "I was just in the art room talking to Ms. Oliver. She's thinking about doing an exhibit of artworks by Canfield students for the public library, and she wants to use one of my drawings."

"That's fantastic, Rosie," Allie said. "Who knows—this might be the beginning of your career as a famous artist."

Rosie chuckled. "Well, I wouldn't go that far. But it is pretty exciting."

She looked at me. "You're awfully quiet, Julie. What's wrong?" Suddenly she gasped. "I know—you don't have any lunch in front of you. The world must be coming to an end!" she said, and giggled.

"Very funny, Rosie," I said. "I got up late and ran out of the house without any lunch money. Do you have any extra I could borrow?"

"Sure," she said, reaching into her purse and pulling out her wallet.

I went and got a ham sandwich and some cookies. When I got back to the table, Rosie, Becky, and Allie, who had been talking intently about something, suddenly fell quiet.

"What were you talking about?" I asked, unwrapping the sandwich and taking a bite.

"Nothing much," Becky said.

Then I started to get mad.

"I don't believe you," I said. "You three were talking about something. It was probably me, because you stopped talking as soon as I came back."

"Julie, it was—" Rosie began in a quiet voice.

"Don't you Julie me," I said loudly. "You were doing it, too."

"Julie, be quiet. Everyone's looking at you," Becky said.

I slammed my sandwich down. I was too angry to eat—and believe me, that was really angry.

"All right, Becky. If you want to be the boss of The Party Line and everything else, you go right ahead. I just don't want to be part of it," I said furiously. "That's just like you. You went ahead and booked a party for a really important day in my life.

Then after I agreed to do the stupid party you tried to tell me how to run my part of it. Now you're telling me to shut up."

I stood up and looked at the three of them. Becky's jaw was set. Allie looked like she was going to cry. And Rosie just looked astonished—she knows I have a temper, but I guess she'd never seen me blow up like that.

All of a sudden I could see myself very clearly. There I stood, like a total idiot, yelling at my three best friends in all the world. And I knew that I wasn't mad at *them*.

I was tired, I was hungry, I was upset because Mark probably didn't think of me as girlfriend material, I was upset because Allie had a date and I didn't—but that had nothing to do with my friends. They hadn't done anything wrong.

But I had. As I stood there, I realized that I had said the most awful things to Becky. I couldn't take them back, and I couldn't imagine that Becky could ever forgive me. I started to tremble. I didn't know what to do.

Finally I picked up my books and ran out of the lunchroom.

The rest of the afternoon passed in a daze. I had spent the remainder of the lunch period crying in the girls' room. Allie and Becky were in one of my classes that afternoon, but they didn't speak to me and I was afraid even to look at them.

When the final bell rang I couldn't face the bus, so I trudged out of school and headed home. It was bright and sunny outside, but I couldn't have cared less—I thought I had lost my three best friends.

"Julie! Julie!"

Rosie came flying up behind me. I looked at her, and tears came into my eyes again.

"Julie, are you all right? I've been so worried about you! Becky and Allie told me that you wouldn't even look at them in class and—Julie, don't cry!"

I sat down on the sidewalk and tried to rub the tears away. It's the one thing about myself that really bugs me. When I'm very upset, I just can't help crying. It makes me feel like such a wimp.

"Rosie, I've ruined everything! They'll never talk to me again and you'll never talk to me again and—and—I'm so *stupid*!" I wailed.

Rosie hugged me tight. "Julie, Becky and Allie know that you're very upset. I *know* they're just as worried about you as I am. After all, you ran out without eating any lunch, and you probably hadn't had any breakfast, either."

I shook my head.

"Well." Rosie let out a soft laugh. "With you, that's enough to make you temporarily insane."

In spite of how rotten I was feeling, I smiled a little.

"Really," Rosie continued, "everything's going to be okay. You'll see."

Just then I heard footsteps, and I looked up. Becky and Allie were standing three feet away from us.

"Julie? C-can we t-talk to y-you?" Allie said timidly.

I nodded, but before they could say anything I blurted out everything I had already said to Rosie. I also tried to explain how bad I was feeling and that I shouldn't blame it on them, but Becky cut me off.

"I know I get a little, well, too pushy sometimes," she said, a little gruffly. Becky hates anything that has to do with messy emotions. "But I'm not mad at you, honest. And I really hope you're not mad at me."

I sniffed and looked at them. The three of them looked so worried that I had to say something to cheer them up.

"Rosie's right, guys. It must have been just hunger that made me feel so weird."

They looked relieved.

"Want to go over to the Moondance? There's some Chicken Parisienne left over from last night," Becky said.

Just then my stomach growled so loudly that everyone could hear it. We all laughed.

"My stomach thinks that's a good idea," I said.

Suddenly I remembered something. "Don't you guys all have stuff to do today?"

"What's more important than best friends?" Rosie asked back. "So my piano teacher has a fit because I'm late. So what?"

I started to protest, but Rosie held up her hand.

"My piano lesson doesn't start until three-thirty," she reminded me. "I have a little spare time."

"And I told Ms. Donner I couldn't make it this afternoon," Becky said, grinning evilly.

"Becky!" Allie was shocked.

"I'll talk to her tomorrow, I promise. Okay?" Becky held up her hand to ward off any further complaints from Allie.

"Well, I never did have anything to keep me busy today," Allie said. "Where's that Chicken Parisienne?"

The four of us started walking toward Becky's. I knew my friends weren't mad at me, but I still felt awful inside. No matter how much I told myself I didn't care about the dance and about Mark, I knew that wasn't true.

Seven

On our way to the mall on Friday afternoon Rosie and I talked about everything except what had happened the day before. I knew my friends were still worried about me, so all Friday I tried to be as cheerful as I could.

As we walked Rosie and I talked about—what else?—clothes.

"There's this incredibly gorgeous beaded jacket at Cinderella," Rosie said. "Beads are in. I was thinking about wearing it with black satin pants to the dance. It would look so awesome."

Rosie's got a sixth sense about fashion. Every time she tells me something's in, I know I'll see it all over my sisters' fashion magazines the next month.

"Sounds neat," I said. "When are you going to get it?"

She shrugged. "Actually, I don't think I can afford it. Even if I saved all my Party Line profits for months, and even if my mom let me buy it at cost, I think it would still be way too expensive."

"Maybe your mom will give it to you for your birthday if you ask," I suggested.

"No way," Rosie said with a sigh. "She thinks it's too sophisticated for me. Hey, I was thinking about what you might wear to the dance. I saw this really neat outfit in Winter's the other day, and it would be perfect for you. It's black and blonds always look totally devastating in black."

I shook my head. "I'm pretty sure my mom wouldn't let me wear black," I said. "Laurel's going through this peculiar phase where all she wants to wear is black, and even though she's fifteen my mom thinks it's too sophisticated for her. There's no way she'd let me wear black."

"That's too bad," Rosie said as we walked into the mall. She stopped by a fountain to tie her sneaker, and I started to walk into Winter's. Their cosmetic counter is right next to the entrance, and it's always a must whenever we go to the mall.

"Wait a second, Julie," Rosie called from outside the store. She pointed down toward the other end of the mall. "Let's get the party stuff first."

I goggled. Rosie Torres wasn't going near the cosmetic counter? Now for anyone else that might not be such a big deal, but as far as Rosie is concerned it was a first. This is the girl who can spot a new shade of plum or burgundy from across the store.

"When we stop back at the makeup counter," I said, "could you help me pick out some new lip gloss?

The Pink Paradise gloss you picked last time is almost gone."

"Oh, Julie, I'm sorry," Rosie said. "I didn't know you wanted to try on makeup today. I promised my mom I'd be back by four-thirty to help her unpack some new clothes the store got in today. I don't think we're going to have time to get the stuff for Ellie's party *and* go back to Winter's. Could we do it next Monday, maybe? I told Allie I'd help her pick out some colors she could wear to the dance, and you could come along."

Fine, I thought. *That's just terrific. Allie has a date to the dance, and so she gets the makeover. What about me? Doesn't it matter what I look like?*

I turned my head and looked very carefully at a display of food processors in the window of Kitchens Deluxe so Rosie couldn't see the tears I was fighting to hold back. *Maybe I shouldn't even bother going to the dance at all,* I thought miserably. *Mark's never going to ask me, and he probably isn't even going to show up. I'm just going to sit home alone forever, like those dorky girls in Heather's class—the ones she makes fun of all the time.*

I knew I was being ridiculous. We'd gotten to The Perfect Party, and while Rosie went in I rubbed my eyes. "Get a grip, Berger," I whispered quietly to myself.

I followed Rosie into the store. We walked down the first aisle, and I picked up a package of paper plates. "These have little elephants on them, so they fit into the circus theme," I said.

Rosie shook her head. "I think we should look for plates in primary colors—bright red, blue, and yellow. Kids really like those colors, and they look more circusy than these pink and blue ones. I mean, the elephants are cute, but they look more like they're for a baby's birthday."

"You're right," I said, and put the plates back. "How about these?" I said, handing her another package with brightly colored pictures of circus wagons and acrobats.

"Perfect," she said.

The matching cups had a picture of a ringmaster who looked just like our school principal. That got us both laughing, and for a while I forgot about the dance.

But as soon as we'd picked out napkins, a tablecloth, party favors, and prizes for the games, we left the mall without so much as stopping for a piece of pizza. By the time I got back to my house, I was down in the dumps again.

When I walked into the house and heard Heather and Laurel laughing in the kitchen, I nearly didn't stop in for a snack. I figured they were probably talking about boys. That's almost the only thing they ever talk about—sometimes it seems as if they've never heard of the Red Sox or the Patriots or anything else real.

I wasn't particularly in the mood to hear about

boys, so I started up the stairs. But my stomach started to growl loudly, so I retraced my steps and headed for the refrigerator.

I was just deciding between a salami-and-cheese sandwich and a slice of apple-carrot cake when my mother walked in.

"Hi, Julie," she said, then she stopped and laughed. "You know, I didn't actually see your face. I just saw someone with their head in the refrigerator and assumed it was you."

I turned around, salami in hand and grinned. My mother's appetite is just as huge as mine. Luckily we both can eat as much as we want and not gain weight. My sisters have never understood how come they have to go on diets when I can eat like a horse.

"Julie, isn't your history test coming up soon?"

Uh-oh, I thought. My mom knows history isn't my best subject.

"Yeah, and I've been trying to study."

"If you need any help, just let me know. I'm sure you can do better than you did on the last test."

I nodded. I had really bombed the last test, mostly because I hadn't studied enough.

"Dinner's going to be a little late today," Mom went on.

"Okay. I've got provisions," I said, and started upstairs.

"Hey, Julie," Laurel called, her nose still in the latest issue of *Saucy* magazine. "You got a phone call earlier. Some guy."

Some guy? I jumped down the last three steps and skidded into the kitchen.

"What guy?" I demanded.

"Mark Frumskool," Laurel said.

"Frumskool?" I repeated. "I don't know anyone with a last name like that."

Laurel looked up with a sarcastic grin. "Dummy! Mark *from school*. He said he'd call you back."

It had to have been Mark Harris!

"Thanks, Laurel. I've got his number. I'll call him right back."

"Julie!" Heather looked up from her bowl of yogurt. "He said he'd call you back. You'll look like such a loser if you go rushing around and call him."

"But he called me," I said. "I don't see why I shouldn't talk to him."

Heather leaned back in her chair. "What do you think he wants?"

I think I turned a bright shade of pink. "Well . . . uh . . . there's this dance at school a week from Saturday, and, uh . . ."

"If he wants to ask you, he'll call you back," Heather said, sounding very certain.

I dragged up the stairs to my room and sat down with my history book open on the desk in front of me. I tried to concentrate on the presidency of James Madison, but I was dying to know whether Mark had called to ask me to the dance. I looked at the clock-radio by the bed at least every two minutes, wondering when he was going to call back.

After what seemed like an eternity but was actually only about half an hour, I decided I was going to call him. I dug around in my desk drawer for the piece of paper with his phone number on it. I left my room and headed for the phone, but halfway there I began to wonder what I would say to him. "Hi, Mark, did you call to ask me to the dance?" didn't seem to be the right thing.

I went back into my room and flopped on the bed. I found myself getting madder and madder at The Party Line. After all, I hadn't even wanted to do the Turner party in the first place, even though I decided to go along with it. But if I hadn't had to go to the mall to get party supplies, I would have been home when Mark called.

My cat padded into the room and jumped up onto my lap. I stroked her head, trying not to think about all the things that seemed to be going wrong. Then I had the most horrible thought: what if Mark had decided to call someone else and invite her to the dance because he couldn't reach me?

Eight

One good thing about having a room that's a converted closet is that it's so small it doesn't take long to clean. Which is what I was doing Saturday morning. Saturdays are when my entire family does chores and takes care of stuff around the house. It might sound like a bummer having to spend Saturday working, but actually it's not all that bad. We wake up early and get almost everything done by lunchtime, and then Dad goes out and gets us two large pizzas with everything on them. Besides, we don't get nagged during the rest of the week.

Laurel walked into my room with the laundry basket. She extracted a set of clean sheets and tossed them on my bed without saying a word. Laurel had babysat the night before, and hadn't gotten to bed until late. She'd been grouchy all morning.

"He hasn't called back yet," I said.

"Who?" Laurel mumbled.

"Mark."

"Oh. Well, it's early. Not everyone's mother runs

the vacuum cleaner outside their door at the crack of dawn."

I wasn't feeling too cheerful that morning, either. Instead of watching TV the night before, I'd stayed in my room with one of Heather's mystery novels. Not that I had especially wanted to read, but I wanted to be near the upstairs phone in case Mark called back. That was so unusual for me that Mom kept coming up and asking if I was okay.

Actually I didn't get all that much reading done. Laurel got four phone calls from her creepy boyfriends, and I gave them the number where she was babysitting. Heather got two calls. I got none.

Finally I'd fallen asleep with the book in my hands. I woke up the next morning with a crick in my neck, but it felt better after I'd taken a really hot shower. I changed my bed, put the dirty sheets down the laundry chute, cleaned out the bathrooms, and went out to help Mom rake the dead leaves out of the garden.

By the time we were done in the yard Dad had come home with the pizzas. I was halfway through my second slice, grumbling because someone had left off the anchovies, when the phone rang.

Mom was right next to it, so she answered.

"Julie, it's for you." She held out the receiver. As I reached for it, she grinned and added, "Don't stay on too long or I'll grab the last slice."

"Hello?" I said into the phone.

"Hi, Julie. Hey, if this is a bad time to talk, I'll call back."

It was Mark! For a moment I couldn't get any words out of my mouth.

"No, no," I finally managed to say. I think I must have yelled it, because everyone stopped eating and looked at me.

"Let me go to the other phone," I said to Mark. I almost knocked over my chair getting up. "Be right back. Mom, will you hang this up when I get upstairs?"

I think I broke some kind of speed record getting up our stairs and to the hall phone.

"Okay, Mom," I said. I waited until I heard the click, then I said, "Hi, Mark."

"Did you get the message that I called yesterday?"

"Yeah. I'm sorry I wasn't here. I was at the mall with Rosie."

"Yeah," he said.

"I've never seen you at the mall," I said, not knowing what else to say. I could have kicked myself. I'd spent the previous twenty hours rehearsing what I would say if he ever called back, and I still sounded like a total jerk.

"Well, I go there sometimes. Mostly to On Track— they have skateboards and stuff there."

"You skateboard? I didn't know that," I said a little breathlessly. I was pretty impressed. You have to be really athletic to be a good skateboarder. "That's so cool."

"Well, you should come watch us sometime."

"Hey, Jon Dolger has that skateboard ramp his dad built in their backyard. I'd love to come over and watch you do all those neat twists," I said.

There was a slight pause on the other end. "Um . . . I'm not that good yet," Mark admitted a little sheepishly.

"Julie," Laurel screeched from the bottom of the stairs, "do you want the last slice of pizza? I gotta go out soon and I have to get the kitchen cleaned up."

"Yeah, just leave it in the fridge," I yelled back. "Sorry, Mark," I said into the phone. "It was my sister."

"I heard her," he said.

"I think my grandmother in Miami Beach heard her," I said.

Mark laughed.

"Sometimes Laurel's pretty unbearable," I said. "Today she's just going to her friend Kate's, so it isn't so bad. But you should hear her if one of us is in the bathroom and she has a date that night."

I almost bit my tongue. I couldn't believe I'd mentioned a date. I was just glad Mark couldn't see my red face.

"I have a sister like that," he said. "More than once she's gone out on a date and left me to clean up the dinner dishes."

That happens to Mark, too? I thought. I began to relax a little. Talking to him wasn't all that tough.

"Anyway, Julie, I've got to get off the phone. We're all going to watch my little brother Steve play basketball. His team's in the semi-finals."

"Oh." I hoped I didn't sound as disappointed as I felt.

"Yeah, so . . . uh, look, I wanted to ask if you were going to the dance next Saturday. I mean, if you *are* going, then, uh . . . well, would you like to go with me?"

I could hear him let out his breath in a rush. Maybe he was as nervous as I was.

"I'd love it." *That* was the truth!

"Cool," he said. "Well, I really gotta go. I guess we can talk some more in school about the dance."

"Okay," I said.

"Later."

"Yeah, see you."

I hung up the phone and bounded down the stairs, taking them two at a time.

When I got downstairs, no one was in the house. Laurel had gone out, my mom had left a note saying she'd gone into the office to take care of some paperwork, Dad was on a ladder pruning trees in the yard, and Heather was just backing the car down the driveway. I was ready to burst with my news about Mark, so I dialed Rosie's number and hooked the phone under my chin.

"Hello," Rosie answered.

"You'll never guess who just called me," I shouted.

"You're kidding!" Rosie squealed.

"Yup, he asked me to the dance," I said.

"Want to go shopping tomorrow?" Rosie suggested. "Winter's opens at noon, and I think my mom can drive us over. Can you be ready at about a quarter to twelve?"

"I'm ready right now," I said.

"Sorry, Julie. I have to put in two hours on the piano this afternoon, or else my piano teacher will kill me for sure," Rosie sighed. "She wasn't real happy with me on Thursday. After I finish that my parents and I are going out to dinner. Otherwise you know I'd drop everything else and go with you."

"I can wait until tomorrow," I laughed. "I sure want you along when I look for a dress. Rosie, did you know that Mark's sister sticks him with the dishes, too, just like mine?"

Rosie laughed. "That's the advantage of having a younger brother or sister. They do all your work for you."

"Okay, Rosie. Go attack that piano. I hope I didn't catch you in the middle of some dramatic Beethoven sinatra or something, but I just had to tell someone."

"That's *sonata*, Julie! I'll see you tomorrow, right?"

"Right."

I hung up and, after checking carefully to make sure the house was still empty, went dancing around the house. I stopped to check out my moves in the full-length mirror in my parents' bedroom.

I nodded at my reflection as I danced a few more steps. "I can't wait until next Saturday," I said out loud. "Paula Abdul, look out—Julie Berger, dancer *extraordinaire*, is ready to go!"

Nine

"We can't spend all afternoon clothes shopping," Rosie said. "I told Becky we'd be on time for The Party Line meeting." We always have a meeting on Sunday afternoon.

"But I haven't seen a thing I like."

"Relax, Julie," she said. "We've only looked in a couple of stores. This takes time. Come on over here." She started browsing through a rack of short knit dresses.

"I brought all my cash," I said. "But just in case, my mom gave me her plastic."

"She trusts you in a clothes store with her credit card?" Rosie said. "My mom would never do that."

"That's because everything looks great on you," I said. "You could grab one of anything."

"Well, not quite." Rosie held a sleeve of a mustard-colored dress up next to her face. Rosie has beautiful olive skin, but I have to admit that color looked awful on her. "I look like I have yellow fever," she said. She dropped the sleeve. "But you're the important one here today. If we can't find you a dress here, maybe we can try some of the small shops in town on Tuesday."

I started to tell her that no way could I afford the prices of those small, exclusive shops. She didn't even let me finish, but steered me toward the back of the department.

"They keep their drop-dead dresses back here," Rosie explained.

"What's a drop-dead dress?" I asked.

"Mom says it's a dress that makes every other woman in the room want to drop dead because they're not wearing it."

"Look." I pointed to a bright-red ruffled, strapless dress. I glanced at Rosie, but I could tell by the look on her face that I didn't even have to bother checking the price tag.

"Julie, that's definitely a prom dress," Rosie said, shaking her head.

"Okay," I said. "But you said blonds look good in red."

"Not that shade of red. It's fine if you want to be a fire engine," she said. "Take a look at this instead."

She pulled a dress from the rack and waved it in front of my face. It was a great blue color and had a sarong skirt.

I tried that dress on, along with at least thirty others, before I heard Rosie squeal. I finished putting a slinky purple one back on the hanger and poked my head out to see what was going on.

"I've found it." She was holding a pile of black material with flashes of pink and magenta. "Remember I told you I'd seen an outfit that would be perfect on you? This is it."

"I don't know," I said doubtfully.

"You've got to try this on."

As usual, Rosie was one hundred percent right. It was a two-piece outfit: a short, flirty black skirt decorated with pink and magenta swirls and topped by a black velveteen jacket. I turned this way and that, and had to admit that I looked great. The black set off my blond hair and fair skin, and the short skirt made my legs look long but not skinny.

Rosie had disappeared while I was trying on the outfit, and soon she came back with a package of black tights and a shoebox.

"These are just what you need to complete that look." She was already opening the package of tights. "I told the saleswoman we were going to buy these even if we didn't get the dress. Okay?"

"Sure, I can always use tights," I said. "But isn't that too much black?"

"Trust me," Rosie said. "Now put them on."

While I was putting on the tights Rosie opened the shoebox and pulled out a pair of black patent flats with magenta piping.

"Aren't those absolutely terrific?"

I tried them on. They were sensational.

"Rosie, I don't believe how great this outfit is!" I said. "But wouldn't this look fabulous on you? I mean, you found it, after all." Even as I said it I was hoping desperately that Rosie had another outfit in mind for herself.

"Hey; we're shopping mostly for you today," she said. "Besides, you look outrageous in that dress. Do you need more convincing? Come on out here."

"Why?" I said, but I followed her out of the dressing room.

"Doesn't she look great?" Rosie said to the saleswoman standing there.

I turned around, playing model for the woman and a couple of customers who were nearby.

"It's just right for you," the saleswoman said.

"Hey, I like that," a girl said. "Where is it? Do you have it in a size nine?"

The saleswoman smiled. "I'm pretty sure that was the last one. We only had a few to start with, so I can just about guarantee you'll be the only person wearing anything like that."

"Mark's going to love it," Rosie said, nudging me in the ribs and winking.

"Yeah, but will my mom love it? I don't think she'll be too thrilled with the idea of someone my age wearing black."

"When she sees how great it looks on, she won't mind at all," Rosie said. "Let's pay for all this stuff now. We don't have a lot of time left, and I found something I want to try on."

Rosie tried on a tangerine-colored rayon top with black triangles for buttons and a pointed collar tipped in black. With it she wore a black knit skirt. As usual, she looked super.

We were lugging our purchases down the mall when Rosie said, "Omigosh. I forgot—we have to get something for your hair."

We were near the drugstore, so we headed in there and went toward the back where they keep the hair accessories.

"Nope. . . . nope . . . no way!" Rosie said as she went through hairband after hairband.

She eyed me speculatively. "You know, maybe you don't need anything in your hair except a few waves," she said.

I snorted. "Good luck," I said. "My hair is as straight as the lines on a piece of notebook paper, and it's too short to put it in rollers."

Rosie smiled knowingly and led me over to another section of the store.

"Gel!" she said, as if she had found the key that would unlock all the mysteries of the universe.

"No Jell-O in my hair. Absolutely not!"

"Ha, ha." She selected a tube. "A little of this in your wet hair, and I can finger-style it into fantastic waves. And this is the best kind, because it won't dry out your hair." She looked at the price. "Eeep!" she said in a small voice. "It's six dollars."

I sighed and handed Rosie my wallet. "Go ahead.

My father said he'd have a stroke if either of us came back from the mall with money left in our wallets."

"We don't want him to have a stroke," Rosie giggled as she took out some bills and handed them to the cashier.

As we walked toward Becky's, I started whistling the latest Bastille tune, "Dream World." Everything was going so well, I felt like I was living in a dream world. But my dreams seemed to be coming true.

Ten

"And wait till you see what I'm going to do with her hair," Rosie said. She was holding up my dress for Becky and Allie to see.

We were all in Becky's attic for The Party Line meeting. The start of the meeting had been officially delayed until Rosie and I had given a fashion show.

"I love the dress," I said. "And I saw one that I'm going to get for our senior prom. It will take me that long to grow enough to keep it up. It's strapless."

Becky let out a hoot.

Allie rolled her eyes. "I can't believe you guys. You go out shopping for a few hours and you come back with your wardrobes planned out for the next five years."

"You always tell us we should be prepared," I said with a grin.

I looked around the room contentedly. It was so nice to be back in our special space with my three best friends, with none of us picking on the others.

I sighed. I hadn't fully realized just how tense our last couple of meetings had been.

Rosie opened another bag. "Look, this is the gel we bought for Julie's hair. I can't wait to try it." She turned to me. "I was thinking—we could probably use a curling iron in your hair and make it even wavier. Becky, can we bring up your curling iron and try it out?"

Becky pointed to the stairs. "There's only one plug up here and it's for the stair light."

"Don't use it," Allie said. "Remember, Becky, when you borrowed David's typewriter and blew all the fuses in the house?"

"Ugh." Becky stuck out her tongue. "I forgot about that. It's a good thing it happened on a Monday when the Moondance was closed, or my mother would have killed me."

"I don't remember that," I said.

"It was before The Party Line," Becky said. "I'd seen a review of the Moondance Café in the newspaper. The food critic hadn't liked our desserts, and so I was going to write a letter to the editor to complain."

"Becky, don't blame the restaurant reviewer," Allie said. "She came the night you decided to experiment with green food color in the whipped cream."

"It tasted exactly the same as the regular white kind," Becky pointed out. "Too bad she wasn't color-blind."

When we'd stopped laughing, I said, "You know,

sometimes I forget that there hasn't always been a Party Line."

"We'll start remembering dates by Party Line stuff. Like my first date was the same time as Ellie Turner's birthday party," Allie said with a smile.

"Yeah, and it'll look great on our history papers," I said. "Columbus discovered America over four centuries before The Party Line."

Allie giggled and dropped down on a pillow. "The first humans on the moon got there mere decades before The Party Line."

"You're a walking encyclopedia, Allie," Becky said.

Allie blushed. "No, I'm not. It's just that I watched a TV show last night about the solar system," she said.

Rosie put the clothes back in the bags. "Allie, do you still want me to French-braid your hair for the dance?"

"You bet," Allie said. She shook her long, wavy brown hair. "Do you really think it will look good?"

"Absolutely. You have such beautiful hair," Rosie assured her.

"Okay, then," Allie said. "But are you sure you'll have time?"

"I can do it in my sleep," Rosie said. "Move over here. I'll do it right now so you can see what it looks like."

"What is this, a beauty salon or a party business?" Becky said good-naturedly. "We'd better get started talking about the party. I have to help out in the Moondance at six."

Allie moved over in front of Rosie, who dumped her bag on the floor and started sorting through the ton of stuff she usually carries.

"I really need a brush, but I can't find mine," Rosie said. "Becky, do you have one?"

"Here," Becky said, tossing hers to Rosie. "But we've *got* to get this meeting started."

"Okay, okay, Madam President," Rosie said.

"Wait—one more thing. Treats," I said, pulling a bag of M&Ms out of my shopping bag. "I figured I might as well spend my last penny on my dearest friends."

Becky handed me a crystal bowl and I poured the candy into it. The edge of the bowl was chipped, but the bowl was still beautiful. It used to sit next to the cash register in the Moondance, to hold after-dinner mints. One day Becky was refilling it and it fell. Her mother said she should have carried it to a table to refill it instead of balancing it on the edge of the cash register, but to this day Becky insists that vibrations from the dishwasher in the kitchen made it fall.

Becky thought the chip on the rim wasn't so bad, but her mother said it couldn't be used at the Moondance and bought a new mint bowl. It wasn't half as nice as the old one, which we got to use in the attic.

Becky put the bowl of M&Ms in the middle of the

floor within reaching distance of us all, and started the meeting. Or at least she tried.

"I love the red ones," Allie said, popping one in her mouth.

"Don't move, Allie," Rosie said, still braiding.

"I like 'em all." Becky crunched down on a handful. "Okay, now that we're all well-dressed, well-braided, and well-fed, can we finally get serious? Mrs. Turner says we can have Ellie's party in their dining room."

"Good." Rosie nodded, her fingers flying through Allie's hair. "We can run streamers from the corners of the room to the chandelier. It'll look like the roof of a circus tent."

"Great idea, Rosie," I said.

"Ooh—ooh!" Becky suddenly exclaimed. "I have the world's greatest idea!"

Allie, Rosie, and I groaned. When Becky says that, either it really is the world's greatest idea or it's a disaster in the making.

"No, really." Becky sat up straight. "Listen. I know the Turners have an enormous St. Bernard dog. Let's turn it into an elephant for the party!"

"Becky," I pointed out patiently, "there's a bit of a difference between a dog and an elephant. About two tons' worth."

Allie giggled. (She finally got one of my jokes!)

"Couldn't we drape a towel over the dog's back, like the blankets circus elephants wear?" Becky pressed. "We could stuff a knee sock with tissues and hang it below the dog's muzzle so it looks like a trunk—"

But Becky didn't get any further with her brilliant idea because the three of us were rolling around on the floor, laughing so hard we were crying. Even Becky finally started laughing.

This feels just like the old Party Line. I thought after we'd calmed down a little.

Rosie fixed Allie's braid, which had come a little undone while we were laughing so hard.

"What do you think?" Rosie said as she twisted a rubber band around Allie's hair. Allie turned her head so we could see the French braid.

"It looks great, Allie," I said.

"Yeah," Becky agreed. "Allie, I think a bow right at the top would really finish it off."

"I've seen some with little ribbons hanging down," Allie said. "Would that be too much?"

"I know what you're talking about," Rosie said. "Mom has some in her shop that have strands of flowers and beads."

"Hey, how many times do I have to remind you that we've got a party to plan?" Becky said with a sigh.

Rosie tossed an M&M at Becky. "May I remind you that our esteemed vice-president and our esteemed secretary have their first dates this Saturday?"

"Duly noted, Madam Treasurer." Becky popped the candy in her mouth. "Now back to the party."

Allie plucked a piece of paper from her jeans pocket. "This is the checklist so far. I'll do a clean copy for Mrs. Turner." She unfolded the paper. "Becky and I will do the clown routine we've been practicing. Rosie, you'll do balloon animals. Julie, you're doing Monkey See, Monkey Do."

She glanced at me. "I mean, if you want to." She must have been remembering how nasty I was the last time we talked about the animal game. She kept her pencil poised over the paper.

"I'll be glad to it, guys. I think it'll fit right into a circus party," I said quickly.

"Check," Allie said, and wrote it on the sheet.

"You're also going to teach them how to juggle, right?"

"Right."

"We got these really neat little stuffed animals for favors," Rosie put in.

"And wait until you see the cake," Becky said, rubbing her hands together.

"It's not made yet, is it?" Rosie asked.

"Of course not," Becky said.

"Well, the way you said that, it sounded as if you'd seen it," Rosie said.

"I saw pictures of the ones Matthew has done before," Becky said. Matthew is the baker who does all the bread, rolls, cakes, and pastries for the Moondance. He gives us a professional discount whenever he does a birthday cake for us.

"What's it like?" I asked.

"It's not a plain old round layer cake," Becky explained. "It's four loaf cakes decorated to look like a circus train. He uses chocolate cookies for the train wheels."

"Yum," I said.

"Definitely," Becky said. "He makes the animals himself, too, from a sugar-cookie dough and animal cookie cutters. He presses them in the frosting on the sides of the cakes, then he uses colored icing to make the bars on the cages."

"Sounds wild," Rosie said.

"I've got everything checked off," Allie said, holding out the sheet of paper. "Rosie, do you want to double-check it?"

"I trust you," Rosie said.

"We all do, Allie," I said.

"That's the great thing about working with your best friends," Becky said. "We can trust each other."

"Mm-hmm," I said, nodding. I was so happy to be eating M&Ms in Becky's attic with my friends. Everything really was back to normal.

I looked over at Allie and Becky, who were conferring over Allie's checklist. I wondered how I could have been so dumb to have been jealous of Allie's date. And I knew I should have known better than to think Becky would have booked a party without considering whether the rest of us could make it.

Sometimes it's really hard getting your priorities straight, I thought as Rosie passed me the bowl of candy. *I was almost ready to put a stupid dance ahead of my best friends.*

I smiled to myself, imagining how much fun the four of us would have at the dance. And I promised myself I'd spend just as much time with Rosie, Becky, and Allie as I did with Mark.

"Julie!"

I looked around to see who was calling my name, and got a large pink pillow in my face.

"Who—what—" I sputtered, then jumped to my feet. No one's ever beaten Julie Berger in a pillow fight!

Eleven

It rained a little on Tuesday morning, but not enough to cancel the after-school soccer practice Coach Piper had scheduled for that afternoon. He had us line up and count off into two teams. Rosie and I always manage to be on the same team, and that day we were on the green team. We put green cloth bands on our arms, donned our shin guards, and jogged out onto the field.

"Hey," Rosie said to me as we ran, "Allie said she went to the mall yesterday and picked out an outfit for the dance. She and Becky are going back today to get shoes to match it. Want to stop by Allie's house after practice and take a look at them?"

"Sure," I said, but my mind was on the game we were about to play. I swear, Rosie can think about clothes no matter what she's doing. I bet she even thinks about them during math tests. It doesn't seem to affect her grades, though.

Halfway onto the field Rosie and I split up, me going toward the middle of the field and Rosie toward the sideline. I was playing center forward because I'm one of the strongest players. Rosie usually plays halfback because she's the fastest runner in the school.

I love all sports. I especially love being out on the field with kids who like to compete as much as I do. I can't understand people who only play because the coach makes them do it. They drag down a team.

Jennifer Peterson was playing center forward on the white team. She's a really good player, too—fast and strong. Jennifer was putting her hair back with a sweatband as she jogged up to me. Her cleats threw up chunks of mud as she ran.

"Yuck. It's goopy out here today," she said.

"It's not too bad," I answered.

Just before Coach Piper blew his whistle to start the game, I turned and gave Rosie the thumbs-up sign. As it turned out, that was the best thing I did in that soccer game. I didn't even survive the first play.

I'm still not sure exactly what happened. Cindy Sawyer kicked the ball to my left and I started toward it, full speed. Jennifer was also running for it. I kicked at the ball as hard as I could with my right foot, but my left foot couldn't get a solid grip on the field. I lost my balance and fell against Jennifer. My leg got tangled with hers, and I went down hard.

Rosie told me later that I didn't look like I was in pain so much as I looked surprised. That's because

I *was* surprised, and also because I didn't feel the pain right away.

When Jennifer and I collided I heard a cracking sound, but it didn't sink in that it was my bone until a searing pain shot through my leg a moment later. Jennifer tried to help me get up, but it hurt so much I think I might have passed out for a second. Next thing I remember, Coach Piper was leaning over me, and the rest of the greens and whites were standing around, looking down at me. Rosie knelt beside me and gripped my hand. Her face was white.

I tried not to cry. Actually, I tried not to scream. I mean, my leg hurt that bad. I couldn't stop the tears from coming, but I did bite back a groan when Coach Piper ran his fingers down my leg.

He pulled off his jacket and put it over me. "Rosie, run to the office and tell them to call an ambulance."

Rosie took off as if he had fired a starting pistol. Coach put his hand under my head, and turned to the kids standing around me. "Someone go to the health office and get a couple of blankets." Two kids raced away in the direction of the school building.

The coach waved his arm. "The rest of you kids move back. Julie's going to be okay."

"Let me stay with Julie," Jennifer said.

The coach nodded. "Just hold on, Julie," he said, "and don't try to move. I'm afraid your leg might be broken."

"Oh, no," Jennifer and I said at the same time.

"I'm so sorry, Julie," Jennifer said.

"It was an accident, Jennifer," the coach said softly.

"I know, but she's hurt so bad." Jennifer bit her lip.

"We d-d-do th-things right," I said. I wanted to crack a joke to make Jennifer feel better, but my tongue didn't seem to be working properly. My teeth were chattering, which was strange because it was pretty warm outside.

The coach looked down at me and frowned. "Chattering teeth aren't a good sign—she must be in shock," he said, and looked up. "Where *are* those kids with the blankets? Hey, you, hurry up," he called.

Suddenly I thought about the dance on Saturday. My leg would probably be in a cast! A picture flashed through my mind of me in my beautiful new outfit and a gargantuan white cast, sitting in a wheelbarrow and being pushed by Mark Harris to the dance. I didn't know whether to laugh or cry.

"Can I do anything for you?" Jennifer asked.

"I'm thirsty," I said thickly.

"I'll get some water," Jennifer jumped up.

"No, no," the coach said. Just then Melinda Wiley came panting up. He grabbed one blanket from her and put it gently under my head. He tucked the other around me. "I don't know what they'll have to do at the hospital, but you'd better not drink anything in case they have to give you anesthetic," he said.

Melinda and Jennifer both gasped.

I didn't. At that moment anesthetic didn't sound so bad; I wished I *could* go to sleep.

Rosie came running across the field just then. The principal was in back of her, but she outdistanced him easily.

Jennifer moved aside so Rosie could kneel by my side. Coach Piper didn't stop her. He knows that she and I are best friends.

"Oh, Julie," Rosie said. She took my hand again and rubbed it. "Are you in pain?"

I nodded. "I'm going to miss the dance."

"Maybe not," Rosie said. "Maybe it's just a sprain."

I shook my head feebly. "The coach says my leg is broken." I tried to smile. "Did you ever hear of a one-legged dancer?" I closed my eyes and turned my head.

I felt someone touch my arm, and I opened my eyes. The principal was kneeling next to me, and he said, "Julie, the ambulance is coming."

Coach stood up and bellowed at the kids who were hovering at midfield. "Game's over for today, girls. You can go to the showers now." They moved a few feet, but didn't turn toward the school.

Then Coach blew his whistle and everyone looked at him. "Get inside. We'll meet again Thursday." Finally they all moved off slowly. Only Rosie, the coach, and the principal were left.

"I'm going to the hospital with her," the coach

said as the ambulance pulled onto the field. "Sarah can take the rugby practice at four."

The principal nodded. "I'll wait for you to come back from the hospital. Call me as soon as you know how she is. My secretary's getting her parents on the phone right now. They'll meet you at the hospital." He looked down at me with a smile. "Now, Julie, don't worry. Everything's been taken care of."

"I'll get dressed and meet your parents at the emergency room." Rosie gave my hand a final squeeze and started running back toward the school building.

By then a whole new crowd of kids had collected. It was only a few minutes after school had ended and most of them had probably been on their way home when the ambulance came screaming onto the field. They stood and stared as the paramedics lifted me onto a stretcher and carried me to the ambulance.

Coach Piper walked at my side, gesturing the kids back. The pain in my leg flared every time the stretcher shifted, and for a minute I thought I was going to be sick. I didn't want to get sick in front of all my friends, and in a moment of panic I worried that Mark was in the crowd. It would have been bad enough for him to have seen me shivering and caked with mud, but if I started barfing he'd probably never want to look at me again.

I didn't see Mark, but Casey Wyatt was standing

by the ambulance. I sure didn't want to see him, so I closed my eyes.

"What a bummer," I heard him say.

For the first time in my life, I agreed with Creepy Casey.

Twelve

"This is just the opposite of the circus," Allie said. "There a bunch of clowns pile out of a small space. Here we try to pile into one."

Rosie and Becky laughed. The three of them had come over right after school Wednesday, and we were all in my room. It was a tight fit to begin with, because my room is so tiny, but when all three tried to get close enough to look at my cast, it got comical.

"I'll sit down here," Becky said, and plunked down on my desk chair. Rosie sat on a footstool next to me. (Mom had brought the stool into my room in case I wanted to sit in a chair instead of lie in bed.) Allie sat very carefully on the end of my bed.

"You know what Julie's dad said when he got to the hospital?" Rosie said.

"What?" Allie said.

"The coach had just finished telling him how the accident happened when they rolled Julie out of the operating room. He went over to her and said, 'I didn't like the play, but it's a great cast.' "

We all laughed, except Allie.

"I don't get it," Allie said, looking puzzled.

I started to explain. "I got hurt in a soccer *play*, and I'm wearing a *cast*," I said, but Allie still didn't seem to catch on.

I sighed. "Never mind." Then I turned to Rosie. "I don't remember much of what happened at the hospital," I said.

"You were pretty much out of it because of the anesthetic," Rosie said. Rosie had ridden her bike to the hospital and stayed with my parents until my leg was put in a cast and I was ready to come home.

"I didn't know they had to operate when you broke a leg," Allie said.

"It wasn't a real operation," I said. "They just put me to sleep for a few minutes while they moved my leg around to get the bones back in the right place. I only had to stay at the hospital until I was fully awake. Then they sent me home with a pain pill so I could go back to sleep."

"Aw, I bet you broke your leg just so you could stay home from school for a week," Becky said, laughing. "How long will you have to wear that cast?"

"Six weeks. Can you believe it?"

The three of them looked at one another.

Allie spoke first. "Julie, I'm going to tell Dylan

that I'm not going to the dance. I'm going to stay with you Saturday night."

"Me, too," Rosie said.

"Me three," Becky smiled. "We're like the musketeers. We might get a little mad at one another once in a while, but in a pinch we'll stand together on our seven good legs." She reached over and squeezed my arm. "Agreed?"

I nodded and laughed, but I was so happy I felt like crying. "You are the best friends anyone could ever have. I'll never get mad at any of you again, I swear I won't. And I don't want you to miss the dance."

"It's a great chance for the four of us to spend a quiet Saturday night together," Rosie said. "After all, there'll be hundreds of dances at school, but how many broken legs will you have?"

"One, absolutely one," I said. "I promise."

"We're really going to miss you at Ellie Turner's birthday party, Julie," Becky said. "You are the best with kids."

"Thanks, Becky, but you know any one of you can lead the games as well as I can," I said.

"Maybe we could," Becky said, "but you really love doing it and the kids know it. Besides, we all have other things to do while you're playing games with them."

"That's right, Julie," Allie said. "It takes all of us to make a party go smoothly."

"That's for sure," Becky said.

Allie blushed. She had missed our last party because she was singing in a talent contest.

"We'll fill in for you this week," Becky said. "By the next party, I'm sure you'll be on crutches."

"I hope so," I said. "The bone doctor—the orthopedist, I mean—is going to talk to our family doctor. Then she'll call me and let me know when I can get up."

"If only she'd let you walk on Saturday," Allie said.

"No chance," I said. "At least that's what my mother said. I was trying to get out of bed this morning—you know, to practice standing on it. I thought if I started today, by Saturday I'd be ready for crutches."

"But Julie, you shouldn't have tried to stand up. You only broke your leg yesterday!" Allie sounded horrified.

I grinned ruefully. "Well, I guess you're right. And my mom agrees with you. When she came upstairs and saw me, she had a bird. She said I'd have only myself to blame if I had to spend the rest of my life with a weak leg."

"Guilt trip," Becky said. "My mom used to tell me that I shouldn't stick my tongue out at David because my face would freeze that way."

"My mother used to tell me that, too," Allie said.

Rosie pulled out a bunch of colored pencils. "It

might not be good to walk on yet but we can sign it, can't we?"

"You bet," I said.

She held out the pencils. Allie took a blue one and wrote her name neatly on the side of my foot. She dotted the *i* with a little circle and made a smiley face in it.

Becky took red, her favorite color, and printed her name on the other side in bold letters.

Rosie stared at the cast before she picked out a couple of pencils and started to draw. When she was finished there was a gold ankle bracelet with my name on it on my cast.

"That's super, Rosie," Allie said. "It looks like the real thing."

"Thanks. It's a little big for the real thing, but as long as it's imaginary I figured, why not?" Rosie drew a big red rose on my heel with an elongated *e* for the stem. "That's my official signature."

She held out her hand. "Can I have my pencils back? I might need them for Saturday's party. If Julie isn't there to do the animal game we're going to have some time to fill. Maybe I can do some cartoons."

"Look, I could go to the party and sit and tell the kids stories," I offered.

"Don't worry about the party," Becky said. "We'll handle the kids. It won't be as much fun without you there, but we'll manage."

"Yeah, it's you missing the dance that hurts," Rosie said.

"You just said there'll be hundreds of them," I said. "Why should missing one hurt?"

"This was the one you were going to with Mark Harris," Allie said.

She had to remind me.

Thirteen

Heather had left her latest mystery novel with me Thursday morning before she went to school. I guessed who had done it in only thirty pages. Maybe I should be a detective after all; that was what I had wanted to be before I decided to be the first female major-league ballplayer. Better yet, maybe I should be a mystery writer and write books with better plots.

Then I picked up a romance novel Laurel had brought me. I skimmed through it, and when I finished it I had the urge to throw it across the room. But my room is so small it wouldn't have given me much satisfaction.

It was the happy ending that made me want to toss the book. I'm not usually against happy endings. In fact, I love them. But I had thought going to the dance with Mark Harris was going to be just like a happy ending. Knowing I was going to miss it hurt more than my stupid broken leg.

The day before, Heather had pressed my new outfit to get all the wrinkles out. (I know, I know. That doesn't sound like Heather at all. But both she and Laurel were acting almost human toward me because of my leg.) When she had brought it upstairs and hung it in the closet, she gave me a present she'd bought me: a comb with a pink ribbon flower on it.

"Even if you can't go to the dance this Saturday, maybe you can wear it and the dress to the next dance," she had said.

As I lay in bed I could see the comb sitting on my dresser next to the tube of hair gel Rosie and I had bought. Looking at them made me want to cry. Instead of walking into the gym with Mark Harris on Saturday night, I would be lying in my shoebox of a room, looking at that big white cast propped up on pillows. It just wasn't fair. Tears started to sting my eyes, but right then I didn't care if I flooded the room.

"Julie, hon, does your leg hurt that much?" My mother stood in the doorway, holding my lunch tray.

"Oh . . . no, Mom." I dragged the sleeve of my pajamas over my eyes. "I was just reading this." I held up the romance novel and reached for a tissue. "It's got a really happy ending." I sniffed.

"Happy endings always make me blubber, too," Mom said. "Anyway, I hate to interrupt your wonderful cry, but I have good news."

"Did the hospital call and say they mixed up my

X-rays with someone else's? You mean my leg isn't broken after all?"

" 'Fraid not." Mom put the tray on my lap and handed me a napkin.

"Well, that's the only news I can think of that would make me happy," I grumbled.

"Try this on for size. Doctor Brady called. She said that you can start using crutches Saturday."

"Saturday!" I almost upset the tray. "Mom, that's great! How come you said yesterday that I wouldn't be walking by then?"

"Because if things didn't work out, I didn't want you to be disappointed," Mom said. "Now eat your lunch. You need a lot of nourishment to heal that bone."

I finished every crumb of my lunch. (Of course, I always do.) Mom brought in a basin of water and my toothbrush so I could brush my teeth. When you have braces you don't skip brushing, even if you do happen to be in a cast.

After lunch I dozed off. When I woke up I couldn't believe I'd fallen asleep in the middle of the afternoon. I hadn't had a nap since before I'd started kindergarten. I must have dreamed about the dance the whole time I was asleep, because when I woke up I was thinking about how I could wear the black tights with my cast.

I struggled for a while to get myself in a sitting position and to adjust the pillows under my leg. I didn't want to holler for my mom unless I really needed her. When I was comfortable I went back to thinking about Saturday night. I probably wouldn't be doing any dancing, but at least I would be there.

Then I had a gloomy thought. Suppose Mark wouldn't want to go with me if I couldn't dance? Maybe the only reason he had asked me was that he had heard I'm a good dancer—or I *was*, before I had to lug around a cast. Maybe he wouldn't want to have to sit on the sidelines next to someone with one huge, fat, white leg. Suppose he called and said he was sorry, but he thought it was dumb to go to a dance with someone who couldn't dance?

I had just about sunk back into the rotten mood I had been in before lunch when Mom knocked on the door.

"Come in," I called. "I'm not sleeping."

Mom opened the door and peeked in. She had that smile on her face—the one she gets when she has a surprise for one of us.

"Guess who's here?" she said.

"Is it Rosie? I thought she had a piano lesson this afternoon."

"It isn't Rosie. And it isn't Allie or Becky, either. It's Mark."

Mark! I was so startled I jerked up in the bed, but my broken leg didn't jerk with me. I groaned.

"Mom, I can't see him like this!"

"How about if I get you your brush? All you need to do is smooth your hair a little. You look fine, honey."

As I frantically brushed my hair, I realized that I was wearing bright-blue pajamas. "Mom, can you get me my Canfield Middle School sweatshirt?" I begged. She got it out of my closet, and I yanked it on over my pajama top. Mom adjusted the blanket over my legs, and then she pushed open the door.

"Come on up, Mark," she called.

It seemed like years passed, but it was only a few seconds before Mark poked his head around my bedroom door. I was so nervous! My mom winked at me as she left.

"Hi, Julie," Mark said shyly. "Does it hurt really bad?" he asked.

"No, it's not too bad," I said.

"Are you sure?" he said with a smile. "I broke my wrist on a Cub Scout camping trip a few years ago, so I know how much it can hurt."

"Well, it's a pain having a cast," I admitted. "And for pete's sake, what do you do when your leg itches?"

"That's easy. Got a hanger?" he said.

I pointed toward the closet. He picked one out and came back over to sit near me.

"See, you unbend a wire hanger, like this. Then you slide it down into your cast to get to the part that itches."

I looked up at him gratefully. "Thanks, Mark," I said. "Now why didn't I think of that?"

He smiled at me, and I smiled back at him. I was waiting for him to break the bad news about not wanting to take me to the dance, but he kept smiling.

"I see a lot of people have signed your cast already." He put his finger on my ankle. "I bet Rosie Torres did that neat ankle bracelet."

"Yeah, she's a great artist."

"Yeah."

We did a little more smiling at each other. "You want to sign it?" I said. "There's a marker on my dresser."

He picked up the blue marker my dad had left in my room the night before, when he signed my cast.

He looked over the names on my cast.

"John Hancock? Who's that?"

"He signed the Declaration of Independence, Mark." We looked at each other and started laughing.

"I know that, dummy," he said teasingly. "Who is it, really?"

I sighed. "That's my dad. He has a weird sense of humor. He asked me if I wanted his John Hancock on my cast. He always calls his signature his John Hancock. Anyway, I said yes, and this is what I got."

While Mark was signing his name and drawing a little picture of a skateboarder, he said, "You're in Epstein's history class, aren't you?"

"Yeah. Who do you have?"

"Berkmans."

"Did you have a test yesterday?" I asked him.

"Sure did. It wasn't too bad. I guess you couldn't take the test because of your leg, huh?"

"Nope," I said. "Not that I mind having the extra time to study. I could really use it."

Mark looked at me. "I'm not too bad in history. If you want, I could lend you my notes. Or maybe we could study together."

"That'd be great," I said. "I'm not exactly mobile these days, but I'm sure my parents would be happy to drive me to the library. If it would help my history grades, they'd probably drive me to New Orleans."

Mark grinned. "Hey, I know that one. New Orleans was the site of the battle the British and the Americans fought in 1814, a few weeks after the War of 1812 officially ended!"

"Just testing," I said with a big smile.

"Wait a minute," he said, laughing. "I thought I was going to be helping *you* study."

Mark's laughing a lot more than he has to if he's going to let me down easy, I thought. I started looking at his eyes, which really sparkled. I'd thought that happened only in books.

He capped the marker and put it back on the dresser. "You like movies?" he said casually as he sat down in the chair next to my bed.

"Yeah."

"Well, seeing as how you can't go to the dance Saturday, I thought maybe I could rent a movie and bring it over." He looked at me and my heart melted.

"I don't mind missing the dance. We'll probably have lots of them. We can catch the next one."

I forgot about my braces and gave Mark the biggest smile I had.

"We don't have to miss the dance."

"Huh?" he said, clearly surprised. "But what about your leg?"

"The orthopedist told me I could be up and around on crutches by Saturday. And to tell you the truth, I was looking forward to the dance. I hate sitting around."

"That's terrific news, Julie," Mark said, beaming. "It'll be neat. You could be the first person at Canfield Middle School ever to dance on crutches."

I giggled. "I'm not sure that's how I want to go down in history."

Mark got up. "All right, then. I'll pick you up Saturday around seven, okay?"

"Okay."

After Mark left I lay back and admired his signature on my cast. Then I grinned. It looked like my story was going to have a happy ending after all.

Fourteen

It was my tenth time walking slowly up and down the hall with the crutches. I felt like I could run a mile, cast, crutches, and all, but I had promised Mom I wouldn't overdo it.

I had been trying to get Becky on the phone, but her line was busy. Allie wasn't home, and there was no answer at Rosie's. I wanted one of them to stop by and pick up my tape player and cassettes for Ellie's party.

I had made a tape especially for the party from a record of calliope music my dad had bought at a garage sale years ago. The calliope music was perfect; it sounded just like old-time circus music.

"Julie, I'm going out. Do you need anything?" my dad called up the stairs.

"Wait a sec, Dad."

I got the tape player and cassettes from my room and dropped them into my book bag. I swung the bag over my shoulder and started down the stairs. On crutches I had to take the steps very slowly and one at a time. Usually, I practically fly down the stairs two or three at a time.

"Dad, would you mind taking me to Ellie Turner's party? I totally forgot to give the tape player and the tapes to Rosie when she came over yesterday, but they really need them for the party. Besides, I'm feeling so much better that I'd really like to go to the party for a few hours."

My father looked at me. "Are you sure you should be doing this?" he asked. "Wouldn't it be better for you to take it easy for a few more days? I can drop the tapes off myself, either at the Turners' or at one of your friends' houses."

"Oh, Dad, please," I begged. "I've been sitting around the house forever and I'm bored out of my skull. It's right between seasons, too, so there isn't even a lot of sports on the tube. After all, how much championship golf can a person watch?"

My father smiled. He's just as big a sports fan as I am, and I guess he could sympathize with me.

"All right. Let me help you to the car."

"Dad, jeez! I can do it!"

My family had been spoiling me rotten ever since I'd broken my leg. Mom had made all of my favorite dishes—lasagna, tacos, stir-fried chicken. Dad had gotten me an enormous baseball encyclopedia. Heather had washed my hair in the kitchen sink, because I couldn't take a shower yet. Laurel had even taken my turns at cleaning up the dinner dishes without saying a word. All that attention was great, but it was kind of weird—sort of like being in the Twilight Zone.

My dad had pulled the car out of the garage, and I hobbled into it. We drove a few blocks to the Turners'. I didn't see any cars I recognized, so I figured I was the first one there.

Mrs. Turner met us at the front door with a surprised look on her face.

"Hi, Julie. Becky told me about your mishap, and I didn't think you were going to be here today. You certainly are dedicated."

I introduced my father to Mrs. Turner. They started talking about me as if I wasn't even there. Mrs. Turner commented on how efficient the four of us had been in setting up Ellie's party, and my father agreed, telling her how terrific The Party Line and me and my friends were. I didn't mind all that praise, but I was getting uncomfortable standing there on crutches with my heavy book bag.

"Dad?" I asked. "Could you grab my book bag for a second? I think I'm going to topple over."

"Sorry, honey," he said, rushing to take my bag.

Mrs. Turner smiled at me. "Suppose I get you a chair and a footstool? That way you can prop your leg up." She disappeared into the living room.

"Now you have to promise me you're going to sit the whole time and not try to lead any games," my father said in a concerned voice.

"What could I do with this cast on?" I said. "Hey, that reminds me of a joke. Once there was a bunch of large spotted cats who preyed on antelopes and other game. One day one of them broke his leg, and since he couldn't run around and chase gazelles and stuff he thought he was going to starve. But then he got a wonderful idea. He went out and rented a jeep. That way he could drive around and jump out at animals as he passed by. Well, naturally, all his cat friends were jealous that they had to run after their prey while all he had to do was work the gas pedal. So what do you think his friends called him?"

My father looked puzzled. "I give up. What?"

"A cheetah!"

My father groaned loudly. "You must get your sense of humor from your mother's side of the family," he said, chuckling.

"Funny, she says I get it from your side," I said with a grin.

Just then Mrs. Turner came back into the dining room dragging a wing chair and a footstool. She set them up and helped me get comfortable. Ellie, who was a bouncy girl with long, dark hair, came downstairs and started telling me about all the friends she'd invited to her party.

Just a couple of minutes after my dad left, I heard the Bartletts' old station wagon turn into the driveway. Allie was the first one to come into the dining room.

She yelled, "Julie!"

Becky and Rosie came running into the house.

"You're here!" Rosie said.

"Now it really feels like a Party Line party," Becky said.

"Becky," Mrs. Bartlett called from the doorway, "I have to get downtown to pick up the spices for tonight's dinner."

"Come on, guys," Becky said. "Let's get the car unloaded."

The first thing Allie, Becky, and Rosie had to do was hang the streamers from the corners of the room to the chandelier. They used blue, yellow, and red crepe paper, and alternated twisted streamers with straight ones. By the time they were done, the Turners' dining room really did look like a circus tent.

While Allie and Becky decorated the table, Rosie sat on the floor next to me with her bag of special long, skinny balloons. She opened her craft book and handed it to me.

"Julie, twisting these balloons into animal shapes is easy. Just follow the directions."

She took a balloon and blew it up. Then she started twisting it in several places. When she had finished, it looked like a giraffe.

"That's fantastic," I said. "I could never do that."

"Sure you can," Rosie said. "Start with the puppy. That's the easiest one."

A few minutes later Rosie had a half-dozen animals done, while I was still working on my first puppy. I kept breaking the balloons when I tried to twist them. Finally I finished one.

"This is pretty sorry-looking," I said. "I think it'll have to be the booby prize."

"It's not bad for your first one," Rosie said. "I used up a whole package of balloons when I was learning. Once you get the hang of it, though, you can do them with your eyes closed."

"These are the best," Allie said when she saw our balloon animals. "Let's hang them from the streamers, then give them to the kids when they go home."

"Great idea," Becky said. "And I think The Party Line should spend one meeting practicing these." She had been looking at Rosie's craft book. "Look at this one," she said, pointing at a parrot made with several different colors of balloons. "Think of all the great party ideas we could come up with using these."

"They're not expensive, either," Rosie said.

"We can talk about that later," Allie said. "It's almost time for the kids to get here."

Everything was a big hit with the kids, from the circus-train cake to the stuffed-animal favors. Becky and Allie's clown routine had the kids in stitches. I was even able to show them how to juggle from my chair. We'd gotten sets of three small beanbags just for the juggling, and until the kids got the hang of it Allie, Becky, and Rosie were busy running around retrieving beanbags.

I cranked up the calliope music while Becky led the kids in Monkey See, Monkey Do. Rosie snapped pictures of the kids pretending to be monkeys, lions, and kangaroos.

The clown sundaes were gone almost as soon as we put them down on the table. My friends took pity on me and brought me my very own clown sundae, which I ate while a bunch of kids clustered around me, touching my cast and asking questions about what it was like to have a broken leg.

When the party was over, Rosie gave every kid an animal balloon with their goody bag, and Allie and Becky led them down the driveway in a circus parade to where their parents were waiting.

When they got back to the house, I was sitting in my chair looking yearningly at the last car of the circus-train cake, which was sitting on a plate on the dining room table.

"Hey, guys," I said, "Mr. and Mrs. Turner said we could eat the rest of the cake."

Becky turned to Allie and Rosie with a mischievous look in her eyes. "Hmm. Do you think we should give her any?"

Rosie tried to suppress a smile. "Maybe Becky's right. Julie just sat there for the entire party. I don't think she deserves any."

"Let's eat it four feet in front of her, so she has to watch it but can't reach any," Allie said in a fake-serious voice.

"Wait a minute!" I yelped. "You can't do that!" All I'd had during the entire party was one measly little clown sundae, and my stomach was growling like a hungry circus lion's.

The three of them laughed. Allie cut a huge slice of cake and brought it over to me.

"This was the best party we ever gave," I said between mouthfuls of cake.

"Absolutely," Allie agreed.

I looked at my watch. "I hate to eat and run," I said, "but my dad's going to be here any minute. It's going to take me a little longer than I'd thought to get ready for the dance," I said, looking down at my cast.

"No problem," Becky said. "You go on home and get ready, and we'll clean up here."

"Then we're going to go over to school. Allie and Becky have to help the D.J. set up, and I have to help put up the decorations for the dance, before we get changed," Rosie added. "I'll be over at your house around six-thirty to help you with your hair."

"I just had a great idea," I said, looking around. "Why don't you all come over to my house when you get done at school, and we'll get ready together?"

Rosie looked at Allie and Becky. "Okay with you guys?"

They nodded.

"All *right!*" I said. "See you at six!"

Fifteen

Before everyone got to my house that evening, I took a shower. Believe me, that's a big deal for someone wearing a cast. The doctor had said not to get the cast wet, but that if I was careful, I could put a big plastic bag over it and take a quick shower.

Mom used almost an entire roll of tape to seal the bag around my leg so that not even a teeny-tiny drop of water could get in. Even so, I think she would have felt better if she had put on her bathing suit and gotten in the shower with me.

She folded a big towel and put it on the bottom of the tub. "Stand on this, honey," she said. "That plastic bag is slippery. And hold onto the grab bar."

I managed to shower without slipping and breaking my other leg. I even figured out how to shampoo my hair with one hand. When I finally got out of the shower and was drying myself, my mom knocked on the bathroom door.

"Your friends are here, Julie," she said. "They're

downstairs. I'm making them some sandwiches, and I'll save one for you."

I put on my robe and clumped downstairs. They were chowing down on my mom's special corned-beef sandwiches. I helped myself to one.

"Hey, Allie, is that your dress hanging on the door?" I asked.

She nodded anxiously. "Do you like it?"

I loved it, and told her so. It was a deep-blue cotton knit, with studs around the jewel neck and the cuffs. The shoulder yoke was suede, and suede fringe swished from the shoulders and down along the out-side of the sleeves.

When we finished the sandwiches we headed upstairs. Heather had already gone out and had vol-unteered to let two of us use her room to get dressed in. Allie and Becky took all their stuff into my room, while Rosie came with me into Heather's room. It was a little bigger, and with my cast I could use the extra space getting dressed.

Rosie dressed quickly in her fabulous tangerine-and-black outfit and swept up her long black hair into a loose knot. By the time she was done, I'd struggled into my new outfit. I'd had to cut off one leg of the tights at midthigh so that they would go on over my cast, and I could only wear one of the great shoes Rosie and I had bought, but as I looked in the mirror I decided that despite the clunky white cast and the crutches I looked pretty good.

"Dynamite!" Rosie said, coming to peer over my shoulder. "Want me to do your hair now?"

She sat me down in Heather's desk chair and spritzed a little water on my hair. Then she put a dollop of gel in her palm and tousled it lightly all through my hair. She combed it smooth and then used her fingers to gently wave my hair.

"Okay, now we're going to let this dry for a while. Then we'll brush through it. You'll see—the waves will still be there, but they'll look really soft."

"Can I see how it looks now?" I begged Rosie a few minutes later.

"Sure," she said, handing me a mirror.

"I look like a nineteen-twenties flapper," I observed, looking in the mirror. The gel kept my hair looking wet, and the waves were close to my head.

"It's cute this way," Rosie agreed. "You can wear it like that to school. But now watch what happens when I brush it out."

"That's great," I said, admiring what she'd done. "You're terrific, Rosie."

"Thanks," she said, smiling at me. "Glad you like it."

"Julie!" Allie exclaimed, coming into Heather's room. "You look gorgeous. And your hair is so cool. It makes me want to cut mine."

I laughed. "Just don't let Rosie do it."

Rosie grinned and made a face at me.

Laurel poked her head into the room just then.

"Becky's dress is just amazing," she said. "She should always wear red."

She moved aside to let Becky come in. Her dress was a total knockout. It was a loose red cotton knit, and it had a wide black leather belt with gold chains on it. Becky pulled the dress out from her hips.

"Mom calls this the red baggie. It's definitely one size fits all. You can borrow it anytime you want, Laurel," Becky said.

"Thanks," Laurel said. "But red is definitely not my color. Tell you what, though, I have a pair of earrings that look like they were made for that dress. I'll be right back." She disappeared into her room.

"I can't believe it," I commented. "Laurel would kill me before she would let me wear any of her earrings."

"I think Laurel is nice," Becky said. "I wish I had a sister. All I've got is David."

"She's only being nice because you're all here," I said. "Well, actually, she's been pretty nice to me lately," I admitted. "I think she feels sorry for me because of my leg."

Laurel came back in with the earrings. They were little gold feathers dangling from tiny onyx studs. There was a matching gold-and-onyx ear cuff for Becky's right ear.

"They look great, Becks," Allie said.

Rosie was busy rummaging around in her makeup bag. She dug out a compact of light pink blush and dabbed a little on Allie's cheeks, then stepped back to examine her work.

"Perfect," she pronounced.

"How's my makeup?" I asked her.

"You're just about done," she said, looking at what I had put on. She added a little deep plum eyeshadow. "There."

Laurel came back to stand in the doorway. "Are you guys almost done in the bathroom?" she asked. "I'm going to take a hot bath once you're gone."

"I thought you were going out with Jason tonight," I said.

Laurel rolled her eyes. "I think sports injuries are going around," she said. "Jason pulled a tendon playing lacrosse and has to stay off his feet for a while. We had plans to go to the Greek place for dinner, but he doesn't feel like going. He called and canceled a little while ago."

Laurel started down the hall, then poked her head back in the door. "A car just pulled up in front of the house," she said. "It's a white Toyota."

"That's Dylan's mom's car," Allie said. "Are we all ready?" Rosie and Becky were riding with Dylan and Allie.

Rosie smoothed on some lip gloss, and grabbed her purse. "I'm ready."

"Me, too," Becky said, looking in the mirror one last time.

Then the three of them came and stood in front of me.

"You are going to be the star of the dance, Julie," Rosie said.

"Come on, you guys," I said.

"You haven't complained at all about your leg," Becky said.

"So we decided to get you a present for being the bravest member of The Party Line," Allie finished. She took a package out of her shoulder bag and handed it to me.

I opened the tiny box. It was a pair of earrings.

"We got them yesterday," Rosie said.

"They match your outfit," Allie said.

Each earring was made of five little gold chains dangling from a golden stud, and each chain ended in a tiny little star. The stars were different sizes and were gold and magenta.

"I love them," I said, looking up at my friends as I put in my new earrings. I felt a wonderful warm feeling all through me. "You guys are the greatest."

I called to my sister, "Hey, Laurel, check out these earrings. Aren't they outrageous?" I bobbed my head and the earrings tinkled gently.

Laurel nodded. "Very nice," she said. "Julie, you look really fantastic. I hope you have a wonderful time tonight."

I could tell Laurel thought I really did look good, and it meant a lot to me. Laurel doesn't usually compliment people—especially me.

"Now get a move on," she said with a smile, handing me my crutches. "Mark's here. I just saw him getting out of the car. It isn't cool to keep him waiting."

As I hopped carefully down the stairs I felt happy and giddy and scared at the same time. I hoped Mark liked the way I looked as much as my friends did.

Sixteen

Mark came to the door just as Dylan's mother drove away with the other kids. He looked incredible. He had on a light jacket, a white shirt with a dark tie, and black jeans.

He'd brought me a gorgeous flower. It was a pink gardenia. I've never smelled anything so beautiful.

"You look great," Mark said. He sounded a little nervous.

"You do, too," I said. "That's a super jacket."

"Thanks."

Just then my parents came downstairs. They started talking to Mark about school and the Red Sox.

Laurel pulled me aside. "You really do look beautiful, kid. And Mom and Dad like him. I can tell," she said, helping me pin the flower to my jacket. "Want me to run out and tell whoever's driving you that you're going to be a few more minutes?"

"Would you? Thanks," I said.

My parents talked with Mark a little more, and

then Laurel came back in with a tall, good-looking guy.

"Mom, Dad, Julie, this is Mark's brother, Rick." I could tell from the look in her eyes that she'd been flirting like crazy with him. I didn't blame her. He was an older version of Mark.

"Julie," Laurel said, "I told Rick that I'm making pizza tonight so you and Mark can have a snack if you're hungry after the dance. And he's welcome to join us if he wants."

At first I couldn't figure out what was going on. Laurel hates to cook more than anything else in the world.

I said, "But Laurel, I thought you—"

"You know I really love to make pizzas," Laurel interrupted me. I finally caught on that she was trying to impress Rick, and I gave her a quick smile.

Mark grinned at Rick. "Pizza is Rick's favorite food," he said.

"Great," Laurel cooed.

"If we're going to eat after the dance then I think we have to go to the dance first, right?" I said.

When we got to the car Mark opened the back door and put his arm around my waist to help me into the car. Right at that moment I almost didn't mind having a broken leg at all. Then Mark loaded my crutches into the front seat, and came around and got in on the other side.

"We're going to meet your friends and Dylan Matthews there, aren't we?" Mark said as Rick drove us toward school.

"Yeah," I said. "I hope you don't mind."

"No, that's fine," he said. "I know you guys are best friends, and I think that's neat."

I settled back in the seat. Mark was cute, fun, liked the Red Sox, *and* he understood how important my friends were to me—he was almost too good to be true!

The gym looked great. That was no surprise, because Rosie had been on the decorating committee. They had crisscrossed streamers in the school colors, green and white, all across the gym. There was a table set up at one end with plates of cookies, bowls of pretzels and chips, and trays of soda. The D.J. that Allie and Becky and the rest of the entertainment committee had chosen was set up with his equipment at the other end of the gym. (The refreshments and the D.J. were paid for with money that the school earned by holding Saturday car washes all year.)

The D.J. had just put on a fast song when we walked into the gym—more accurately, Mark walked and I hobbled. As we walked around the room heading for some tables and chairs set up near the refreshment area, I saw Allie and Dylan already dancing. Allie spotted me and gave me a quick wave.

Rosie and Becky were seated at one of the tables talking to a bunch of kids. When they saw me, they all moved over, and Becky brought over three chairs—one for Mark, one for me, and one for my leg.

Jennifer Peterson was with them, and she gave me a wide smile.

"I'm *so* glad you're here, Julie," she said. "How's the leg?"

"It's doing pretty well," I said.

"I feel awful about what happened," Jennifer said anxiously. "I really didn't mean—"

She looked upset, so I said quickly, "Oh, Jennifer, it was an accident. Even the coach said so. I mean, the field was muddy, and we were both running at top speed, and when I slipped, you just happened to be right there." I smiled. "Next time we'll just have to synchronize our timing."

She laughed. "I'm glad you don't hold it against me."

The kids all wanted to inspect my cast and sign it. While everyone was signing, I looked up and saw Casey Wyatt saying something to Mark. Mark frowned at him, and Casey shrugged. Casey is such a jerk and Mark is so terrific that sometimes I have trouble believing they're really cousins.

Casey came over to me and said, "Hey, Metal Mouth."

I sighed. I figured I should be polite to him, because he was Mark's cousin.

"How's it going, Casey?" I said.

"You do pretty good on those sticks," Casey said.

I could hardly believe it. Casey had said something to me that wasn't rude and disgusting?

Just then the D.J. put on another fast song. Casey smirked.

"Wanna dance?" he said.

I couldn't help grinning. I shouldn't have worried: good old Creepy Casey was still with us.

"Sorry, Casey," I said. "You couldn't keep up with me, and I wouldn't want to embarrass you in front of everyone."

Mark came over with a plateful of pretzels and a couple of orange sodas.

"Hungry?" he asked me.

I nodded.

Andrew Piatelli, a really tall boy in the eighth grade, asked Rosie to dance. She flashed him her brightest smile and went off into the crowd. I don't think we saw her more than five minutes at a time after that. Rosie loves to flirt, and every time I looked up she was dancing with a new boy and looking like she was having a great time.

After the next song ended, Allie and Dylan came over to sit with us for a while. A few other kids came over, and we started talking about whether the school might have another dance before the year ended.

Becky was sitting next to me, and so I saw the surprise on her face when Paul Schneider, another eighth grader, leaned down and asked her to dance. She nodded and followed him onto the floor.

Four songs later she came back without Paul, who had gone to get them some sodas.

I stuck my head next to hers and whispered, "You and Paul seemed to be doing a lot of laughing out there."

"Yeah," Becky said. "He was telling me some hilarious stories about when he tried to earn money last summer by walking dogs."

"Is that so?" I said. "I think he likes you."

Becky looked scornful. "Oh, come on. We were talking about *dogs*. That's not exactly a romance-packed subject. Where's Rosie?" she added, looking around.

"She went to the girls' room," Allie said.

"There she is." I pointed to the doorway, where Rosie was standing talking to a couple of girls. She came over and flopped down into the chair next to me.

"This is awesome, totally awesome."

"I think you've danced with every boy in the school," I said.

"Not Mark," Rosie said. "This is the first time he hasn't been by your side all night. Where is he, by the way?"

"He said he wanted to go look at the D.J.'s equipment," I said. I scanned the other end of the gym. "There he is, talking to him," I said, pointing.

We talked for a few minutes about who was dancing with whom, and then Mark came back.

"Let's dance, Julie," he said.

"Uh, Mark, I have this little problem," I said, pointing to my cast.

"Oh, that's okay. This is going to be a real slow number. You won't even need your crutches."

He must have made a special request to the D.J., because just then Vermilion's "No One Like You" filled the air. It's a perfect song for slow dancing.

Mark helped me get up, and we moved a step or two away from the table. He came closer to me and circled me with his arms, steadying me so I wouldn't lose my balance. I put my arms around him and closed my eyes as we swayed to the music.

When the song ended we stopped moving and I looked into his deep-blue eyes. He smiled and murmured, "Thanks for the dance." I nearly melted.

He helped me back to the table and sat with me for the last song of the dance. When the music was over and Mark had gone off to call his brother Rick for a ride, Rosie came over to me with her eyes sparkling.

"Julie, you and Mark looked totally cool on the dance floor. And you didn't even need your crutches!"

"If I could always feel like this, I'd never have to use crutches again," I said dreamily.

"Feel like what?"

"Like I'm floating."

Seventeen

On the way back home Mark and I talked about the dance a little, but we didn't say much. I felt really comfortable with him, not like I had to fill up every second of the ride with nervous talk.

When we got back to my house I recognized the Grays' car backing out of our driveway. Allie had called her parents for a ride back, but before we left the dance we had agreed to meet at my house for some of Laurel's pizza. Dylan couldn't come, Allie said, because he and his family had to leave early the next morning to visit relatives out of state.

Allie, Becky, Rosie, and Laurel were already sitting around the kitchen table when Mark, Rick, and I walked in.

"Smells good," I said, not a little surprised. Not only does Laurel not like to cook, but when she does the rest of my family prepares for an evening of indigestion.

"Thanks," Laurel said, getting up to take Rick's jacket.

"Here," I said, tossing her my coat with a wink. She caught it without saying anything, but crossed her eyes at me when no one else was looking.

The pizza was actually pretty good. (I found out the next day that she had called our aunt in New York for her famous recipe.) While we ate it we talked about the dance that night, and Laurel and Rick talked about how different high-school dances were from the middle-school ones.

"You mean they usually have live bands?" Rosie said. "Great!"

"Maybe by then I'll be out of this cast," I joked.

"I sure hope so," Rick said wryly. "I don't want to spend the rest of my life driving you and Mark around."

I looked at Rosie with wide eyes. Had Mark told Rick that he wanted to go out with me again?

We finished the pizza, and Rick said, "Hey, Mark, we'd better get going. It's kind of late." He looked from Mark to me and back to Mark again, then added, "I'll go warm up the car."

He got up to leave, and said casually, "Laurel, want to come outside for a couple of minutes? It's really nice out tonight."

"Sure," Laurel said, and followed him out the door to the driveway.

"Uh . . ." I said.

Rosie, wonderful person that she is, jumped in. "My parents said they'd pick us up here and take you guys home," she said to Allie and Becky. "Let's go call them." She started out of the kitchen.

"But the phone's right here," Becky said.

Rosie yanked on her arm. "This is the one that doesn't work too well, *remember*? Let's go upstairs and use the hall phone."

Mark and I were alone in the kitchen. All of a sudden, with the date coming to an end, I felt awkward.

"I hope it wasn't too weird for you, going to a dance and not dancing," I said.

"I didn't mind," he said. "Besides, we did dance." He grinned at me. "You're pretty hot out there on the dance floor, Berger."

I had to laugh. "Yeah, it's the latest dance craze. 'Wobble and Clunk,' it's called."

"Seriously, Julie, I had a great time." Mark looked at me with those blue eyes.

"Me, too."

We were silent for a few seconds. I wondered what he was thinking, whether he wanted to see me again. Finally I collected all my courage and, with my heart pounding, said as casually as I could, "So, is your offer to help me study for that history test I have to make up still good?"

"You bet," he said quickly. "Uh, how about next Wednesday? Maybe we could go to the taco place after school and have something to eat, too. I never could study on an empty stomach."

"Me neither."

We looked at each other for a few seconds, grinning like idiots.

"Well, I really should go," he said at last.

"Okay."

I struggled to push myself out of my chair, and Mark laughed. "You don't have to get up. I know where the front door is."

I sank back down gratefully. "Thanks, Mark. I'm just really beat right now."

At the kitchen doorway he turned and looked at me. "See you in school Monday," he said, then he disappeared.

"Bye," I said quietly. I was so happy I felt as if my heart were going to bust right out of my chest.

No sooner had the door slammed than Allie, Rosie, and Becky came thundering down the stairs and into the kitchen.

"Well?" Rosie demanded.

I couldn't help smiling. "We have a study date for Wednesday. And he said he had a great time!"

"You look like you did, too," Allie said.

"You got that right," I said happily.

"Well, Laurel had a good time tonight, too," Rosie said with a wicked smile. "We just happened to look out the front window and saw her kissing Rick."

"Yuck!" Becky said.

I laughed. "Sounds like Laurel all right."

Allie had a dreamy look in her eyes. "I wonder what it's like," she said.

"What?" Becky demanded.

"Kissing someone, dummy," I said to Becky.

"Yuck!" Becky said again.

"Oh, I don't know. I suppose it depends upon who it is," I said.

We were quiet for a few minutes. Then Rosie said, "I had a really great time tonight. The music was terrific and I loved dancing and everything, but I especially liked spending time with you guys. And I like Mark and Dylan," she added to me and Allie.

"I do, too," Becky said. I was sort of surprised to hear that from Becky. I sometimes wondered if she thought we were really stupid for being interested in boys.

As if she had read my mind, she continued, "I mean, they seem like real people. And it's not like they tried to drag you off for the entire dance so we couldn't talk to you. They seemed like they enjoyed hanging around with the four of us."

Rosie nodded. "I got that feeling, too. And you know something? I'm really glad. Remember after Allie's surprise party we talked about how we might start going out with boys and stuff? We said we'd never let it get in the way of our being friends, and it hasn't."

"You're right, so far it hasn't been a problem," Allie said thoughtfully. "But I still think we have to pay attention and make sure that it doesn't ever become a problem."

Allie is so smart about these things, I thought. Out loud, I said, "I think Allie's right. Sometimes I hear

Heather and Laurel discussing how one of their girl-friends just seems to have dropped out of sight because she's started dating some boy. I hope that never happens to us."

"Don't worry, Julie. I don't think any of us are going to fall into the Black Hole of Dating," Becky joked. She can always be counted on to say something funny whenever our conversation threatens to get too mushy.

Rosie yawned. "I've just about had it, guys," she said. "What with Ellie's party, decorating the school gym, and the dance, I think I could fall asleep right here on the table."

"When are your parents coming?" Allie asked.

Rosie checked her watch. "They should be here any minute," she said. Right on cue, the doorbell rang.

"Bye, Julie," Allie said, coming over to give me a hug. "I'm glad you made it to the dance."

"See you guys tomorrow for the regular Party Line meeting?" I said.

Becky nodded. "Just you wait until you hear my latest great idea," she said sleepily.

"Ack!" I yelled, throwing an apple at her from the bowl on the kitchen table. "It'd better not involve turning a dog into an elephant or a camel or a fish or—"

Becky's retort was cut off as Rosie and Allie dragged her out the door.

I went upstairs and hung up my new outfit. I eased

myself into bed and propped my cast in a comfortable position. I turned out the light and stared at the dark ceiling for a few minutes, thinking about all the great things that had happened that night.

"Not bad, Berger," I said softly to myself, and drifted off to sleep.

SPECIAL PARTY TIP
Julie's "Borrowed" Ice-Cream Clowns

I admit it: I borrowed this idea from Becky. But I think it's better to borrow a good idea than spend a lot of time and trouble coming up with a new one. It sounds lazy, but it's really very practical. Besides, Becky's one of my four best friends, so I know she won't mind.

Ice-cream clowns are a big hit with children, and I've even been known to eat them up myself. They're easy to make, too.

Shopping List: Ice cream.
Sugar cones.
Whipped Cream. (You can use either kind: canned or homemade. If you're making it yourself by whipping heavy cream, just be careful not to whip it too much. If you do, you'll end up with butter!)
Any kind of small round candies. (You can even use raisins if you like.)
Red licorice.

Place a nice round scoop of ice cream in a bowl. Squiggle whipped cream around it as if you were making a big fluffy clown collar. This is easier to do with canned whipped cream, but homemade tastes better. If you're using homemade, just dab small spoonfuls all around to get the same crinkly look. Then use the candies to make the eyes and nose, and use the licorice to make the mouth. (If you're a little messy like I am, you may want to put the candies in *before* you add the whipped cream.) Top everything off by sticking an ice-cream cone "hat" (pointed side *up*), on top of the ice cream scoop and *voila*! One ice-cream clown.